HARTSVILLE'S SEAL HEROES

The SEAL's Convenient Wife

The SEAL's Surprise Baby

The SEAL's Instant Family

The SEAL's Pregnant Roommate

The SEAL's Treatment

The SEAL's Hookup

The SEAL'S Surprise Baby

HARTSVILLE'S SEAL HEROES BOOK TWO

USA TODAY BESTSELLING AUTHOR

LESLIE NORTH

BLURB

Navy SEAL Anderson Park and agency operative Violet DiPaula didn't like each other, but that didn't diminish the spark between them. On a mission together in Russia, they gave in to the red-hot chemistry between them. Anderson is always prepared, but nothing could have prepared him for returning from a mission more than a year later and learning that their one night of passion left Violet pregnant. Anderson's good at most things, but he knows he'll be a lousy father. Now Violet and his five-month-old son are in danger, and he can't abandon them. As much as Anderson knows he's not cut out for family life, he can't avoid his protective instincts toward Violet and Nate. Before he knows it, he also can't keep his heart from feeling things he's never felt before…

If it were just Violet on the run, she'd be fine. But she has Nate, and that changes everything. Violet has always taken care of herself, and it's no easy task allowing Anderson to help her and their son. She doesn't *need* a man, but the safe house is her undoing. It just all seems so cozy, and having a sexy SEAL around morning, noon, and night isn't the worst thing that's ever happened. No matter how many times

Violet reminds herself she doesn't need a thing from Anderson, as the danger increases and they must rely on each other more and more, she finds herself falling hard. If they survive the Russian mob, can their love survive as well?

MAILING LIST

Thank you for reading "The SEAL's Surprise Baby"
(Hartsville's SEAL Heroes Book Two)

Get SIX full-length novellas by USA Today best-selling author Leslie North for FREE! Over 548 pages of best-selling romance with a combined 2748 FIVE STAR REVIEWS!

Sign-up to her mailing list and get your FREE books:

www.leslienorthbooks.com/sign-up-for-free-books

CONTENTS

1

"What?" Anderson said, trying to keep his mouth from hanging open. He couldn't have heard her correctly. Maybe the sound of the breeze moving through leaves was messing with his hearing. Had she just declared that the baby in her arms was his?

"You have a son," Violet repeated, smoothing a hand over the boy's hair. "His name is Nate."

"Nate." Anderson spoke the word slowly, waiting for his brain to catch up with Violet's announcement.

"Nathan Anderson DiPaula," she said. That was her last name. Instinct made him want to argue the point. If the kid was his, the boy's name should be Nathan Park.

No. Wait a minute.

"He can't be mine. I never…" Never what? Never let my swimmers out without a safety net? No SEAL worth his salt did, in Anderson's opinion. He didn't have unprotected sex—ever. But he looked at the boy with his dark hair and eyes and wondered. Was it possible?

"Do you mind if we come in?" Violet asked, glancing behind her. "I don't want to talk about… certain things standing on your porch."

"Yeah… sure," Anderson muttered and stood aside to let her—and the baby—by. He'd been enjoying some time alone, recovering from his last mission, when Violet had unexpectedly knocked on his door. He walked ahead of her into the living room, gesturing to the couch he'd been napping on. Any sense of peace or relaxation he'd found had vanished the instant he saw her.

They'd parted fourteen months ago at Ramstein Air Base in Germany after an emergency extraction from the assignment they'd been on together in Moscow. When he'd thought of her since, it had been with a sense of irritation. Everything about her got under his skin. Her fearless attitude, her cool intelligence, her sexy body.

Having a baby hadn't changed that much. Her slim-fitting jeans and pink tank top revealed the curves he'd been unable to resist that last night in Russia. A fateful night, if what she said was true and the kid was his. He focused on the boy. He had fine dark hair that fell over a high forehead and eyes darker than his mother's. Hers always seemed to glow with a sort of inner light.

The baby's chubby hands reached out and yanked on Violet's chestnut hair.

"We talked about this, little man. No pulling Mama's hair," she said as she smiled at Nate and gently removed the locks from his fist. "Let me find you a toy." With one hand, she dug in the bag she'd dropped at her feet. "How about this?" She offered the boy a book made from fabric.

"Does he like that?" Anderson asked, finding his voice.

"It's a favorite. I think he'll be a scholar."

"Like his mother," he said. She was one of the smartest people he knew. He hadn't always liked her, but he'd respected her ability to analyze data and make projections. He was good at that, too, but her skill far surpassed his.

"And Daddy," she added, shooting him a look.

Anderson's scholarship was hard won, since he'd come from damn close to nothing. He'd risen above his beginnings, doing more than anyone expected from him, but shit, had he ended up just like his parents with an unplanned kid? He had to get his head around the idea of having a baby.

"How'd this happen?" he blurted out.

"The usual way, Anderson. We had sex." She gave him a look that said, *Try to deny it*. "Do I have to explain the biology?"

"I get that part, but I also know there was a condom involved." He wasn't the type to take risks, ever. Not even back when he'd been a randy sixteen-year-old—and certainly not a year and change ago.

She lifted her shoulders an inch. "Ninety-eight percent effective when used correctly, according to the sources I checked. That leaves a two in one hundred chance."

"Thanks, I can do the math," Anderson said, working to keep the sharpness from his voice. "How old is he?"

"Five months. I just got confirmation a few days ago that you were back in the States," she added, as if anticipating his next question.

"Right." Anderson couldn't stop studying the child, looking for signs of himself in the set of his mouth and his laugh as the baby turned the pages in the book.

"You were gone on a long deployment, from what I could find out," she continued.

"You checked?" With her security clearance and connections in the intelligence world, she would have been able to find out that he was deployed. She might even have uncovered where he'd been, but she'd made no move to contact him. At least, not that he knew of.

"I did," she admitted as she lowered the boy to the floor so that he sat supported against her legs. He seemed able to sit up pretty well on his own. Maybe he was an advanced little guy, Anderson thought, and then the kid stuck half the cloth book in his mouth. Guess not.

"So you waited for me to be on leave to drop this bomb," he said, watching as she offered the baby a set of plastic keys in exchange for the now-wet book. She tilted her face toward Anderson before speaking.

"I waited because I wasn't sure I'd tell you at all." Those eyes that seemed to have their own light stared into his. "I don't need you. I can raise him on my own and give him everything a child needs."

"Except a father," he pointed out, fully aware of the irony of his words. His father had been a crook and a wannabe con artist. Not exactly daddy-of-the-year material. Anderson's grandfather hadn't been any better. Fatherhood wasn't in his genes.

"I grew up without one," Violet retorted. "It's never held me back."

That much was true. She'd never been daunted by anything. Not that he'd seen. But raising a kid on her own had to be tough.

Did that mean he wanted to be involved? Hell, he didn't know the answer to that.

"So why'd you show up at my door?" he asked, trying to understand her motive.

"I decided you had a right to know," she said, touching the boy's head. "And he's so sweet. I couldn't live with myself if you didn't have the opportunity to experience that." She cleared her throat, and he felt there was something she wasn't saying. "So that's why I'm here."

He believed her, but something didn't add up in his head. He let a minute pass in silence while he analyzed her words. Then he said, "You would have known you were pregnant before I was deployed on my last mission."

"That's true. I suppose I should explain a little more about that," she said. "I've never been regular, you know what I mean?" He nodded, not wanting to get into a discussion of female issues. "So I was almost five months pregnant before I let myself believe it. When my clothes stopped fitting, I could no longer deny the reality, so I took a test and saw the doctor."

"You weren't sick?" Didn't women know these things? There were signs, or so he'd always heard.

"Not a day. And I wasn't tired either, like so many women say they are. It was an easy pregnancy." She lifted the baby back onto her lap. "Anyway, by the time I came to terms with it, you'd shipped out— and I'd thought that was just as well, since we don't..." Her mouth closed into a firm line.

"Get along," he supplied. Both their working and personal relationships had been infused with tension, some of it sexual, but much of it a battle of wills.

"Right." She swallowed, a surprising show of nerves on her part. "But I'm here now to give you a choice. Your son can be part of your life or not. If you decide you want nothing to do with him, I'll never bother you again."

Anderson started to say *If he's mine*, and stopped himself. He had no reason to doubt her assertion, and the time frame worked. The kid... Nate... was his. Did Anderson want to be a father? He had never planned on it. But he also didn't shirk his responsibilities.

But, Jesus, it was a hell of a decision to be asked to make out of the blue.

He'd seen enough careless and irresponsible behavior from his own parents to know he didn't want to emulate that. But could he do this? Could he be a dad? And what would that mean for him and Violet? He saw a future fraught with battles, which was not how he wanted to live.

But he'd fathered a kid, and that meant something. He'd pay child support. The Navy would help him set that up. Beyond the monetary, though… he didn't know. His mind swirled, refusing to go in any coherent direction.

"Got it. Message received," Violet said and got to her feet, interpreting his silence as refusal. She slung her bag over her shoulder and cuddled Nate close to her body.

Anderson had seen her in slinky dresses meant for nightclubs and in business suits, but she'd never looked more beautiful than she did then. Her clothes were casual, her hair mussed, but her face, body, and attitude got to him just as much as they always had.

And he knew that he didn't want her or his son to walk out his door. Not until he'd had a chance to think this through.

"Wait," he said, jumping up and moving to be in front of her. "You've got to give me a little—"

The sound of bullets from an automatic weapon suddenly filled the air. Instinct made Anderson wrap his arms around Violet and Nate and take them to the floor with him. Everything in him said to protect them above all else. He landed on his back, taking the brunt of the impact, and then rolled with them to use his body as a shield.

The hail of bullets ended, leaving a car alarm blaring in the street. He eased up, checking his surroundings.

"Is he…?" For the first time, Anderson touched his son. It was inadvertent, a simple hand to the boy's cheek, but it was soft, warm, and captivating.

"He's fine," Violet said, her voice shaky. "What happened?"

"Not sure. Stay down," he said as he rose into a crouch and made his way to the window. He looked through the glass pane and saw the sedan Violet must have arrived in riddled with bullet holes. A rock hurtled toward the house as a black SUV peeled out and careened down the road, almost hitting Anderson's mailbox. He took another minute to scan the area before standing. When he did, he bumped into Violet. Why had she joined him at the window? He should have known she wouldn't stay still—but the kid.

Anderson turned. Nate lay on his back on the carpet, moving his limbs and babbling to himself, undisturbed by anything that was happening.

"There's a note," Violet said, pointing through the window to where the rock had landed on his porch.

"I'll get it." He didn't bother to tell her to stay in the house. It was a waste of breath.

Anderson stepped onto the porch to retrieve the note. Once he was back inside, he unfolded it and scanned the words. Violet leaned in to see it, her hair brushing against his arm.

"My God," she muttered in Russian, speaking in the language of the note.

His language skills were on par with hers, and he had no trouble understanding the threat.

Next time, you'll be in the car.

"I didn't think…" She made her way back to the couch, scooped up Nate, and sat down heavily.

Didn't think what? Violet was shaken… but not surprised. What was going on? He studied her. Her head was bent over the baby's, and her body seemed to be folded inward. He needed to break through the walls she was constructing and get her to talk.

"Let me take him," Anderson said, walking toward her and reaching for his son. His request jolted her.

Violet glanced up, her eyes unfocused for a second, before handing Nate over. Anderson felt awkward for a minute as he tried to mimic how she'd carried the baby, but he soon figured out to rest Nate against his chest. He paced the room, keeping an eye on the street out front, but he didn't expect them to return so soon since they'd delivered their message. "Explain what you know," he said. "Don't leave anything out."

"There was a data breach two months ago," she began after the tiniest hesitation, "not long after I went back to work following my maternity leave." Her job for a government agency wasn't the kind she could discuss with most people, but he already knew about it. He'd been her protector, a glorified babysitter, really, while she'd been on assignment in Moscow.

"The leak had to do with information you collected in Russia," he guessed.

She nodded. "It revealed some of the surveillance and analysis and who conducted it."

"And your bosses didn't react." That surprised him. They were usually protective of their assets, and that's how they would view Violet.

"It was deemed minor with minimal exposure, but…"

"But what?" he demanded, keeping his voice level. Nate seemed to be dozing, cuddled into him, and he didn't want to spook the boy.

"I've had a few strange incidents since," she said, her fingers twisting the edge of her shirt. "Little things. Someone following too close behind my car. An unexpected package on my doorstep."

"What was in it?" Anderson paused in his pacing.

"Russian nesting dolls." She gave him a wry smile. "A warning, no doubt. I think someone's toying with me, but I don't know why."

The bullet-filled hunk of metal on the street was way past a warning. Fortunately, he lived on a country lane outside town and had no immediate neighbors. No one would be freaking out and calling the police. At least not yet. He had a little time for his mind to tick over what he knew. He didn't like any of it.

"We need to get out of here," he said after a minute spent analyzing their best course of action.

"What? Now?" She stood, her body reacting to his suggestion.

"Yeah," he said, "unless you want to wait around for them to come back." She was too smart for that not to be obvious to her.

She glanced out the window. "I should report this to my supervisor."

"Did you report the other things?" he demanded.

"Of course." She reached into her bag and pulled out her phone.

"And what did they do?" he asked before she could dial.

"Nothing, which didn't really surprise me—who knows; they might have more information than I do." Her fingers stilled over the buttons. Since her area of expertise was risk analysis, he found it odd that anyone had doubted her assessment. "The threat seemed as though it originated from a minor source with minimal exposure, same as the original data breach. I've followed the usual protocols for enhanced threat, though."

How much more complicated was that with a child to care for? Anderson didn't want to think about it. He would later, after they were in a safe location.

"My car's in the garage," he said, ready to take action. "Let's roll."

"Wait. I can't go on the run with a baby. All I have for him is what's in this bag. Let me go home and—"

He cut her off. "No. Your place isn't going to be safe." He knew he was right about that, but fleeing a threat with a baby—with his son—wasn't the way he wanted to spend his first day as a dad.

"I…" She only hesitated a couple of seconds; he could see her evaluating the situation in her head, assessing risks and options. "Okay. You're right." She grabbed the bag and took Nate from Anderson. "Car seat?"

"What?" It was his turn to be surprised.

"Kids have to ride in a car seat for safety," she explained. "We'll need to get it from my car if it's not damaged."

He wanted to argue that their situation was inherently unsafe, but her jaw had a stubborn set he remembered well. "I'll get it. You can reach the garage by going through the kitchen."

He pointed the way before pulling jackets from his hall closet and stuffing them into a tactical bag he always kept packed. A minute later he yanked the door of the bullet-riddled car open to retrieve the car seat. He had no idea how to manage the thing, but he managed to detach it and hauled it to the garage.

"Let me," she said, taking it and quickly strapping it down while he held Nate. He watched her run her finger over a notch in the plastic where a bullet had sliced through. "Good thing he wasn't..." She didn't need to finish the sentence.

"We need to move," Anderson said to hurry her along. Thirty seconds later, he backed out of his garage and headed in the opposite direction from where the black SUV had gone. He didn't want to run into whoever had been at the wheel with Violet and Nate in the car.

The problem was he had no idea where the hell they were going.

2

———————

Fourteen months earlier

The techno music thumped loudly in the neon and glass of the club as Anderson scanned his surroundings. Violet's plan was simple: They would look like an amorous couple enjoying a night out, while getting some shots of a mobster who frequented the club. Anderson was glad to be out of the apartment he shared with Violet as part of their masquerade. He hated being pent up and idle. Watching Violet analyze data wasn't doing it for him.

They took to the dance floor as soon as they entered the club. It was no hardship for Anderson to dance with Violet. They'd been dancing around each other enough over the past weeks while working together in Moscow. Butting heads, fighting for control. It was almost a sexual release to be so close to her, both of them bumping and grinding.

He had his phone out while they moved to the music, pretending to take pictures of her as she danced. She made a memorable photograph in the barely there dress that exposed the tops of her breasts and ended an inch below her ass. He playfully held up a finger to indicate he wanted one more shot. Anyone watching them would interpret it as his asking her to pose. She took his cue, pouting her red lips and running her hands down her body in a seductive move.

He saw her eyes widen for a split second before returning to her previous sultry expression. She moved closer, her fingers going into his hair as she leaned in.

"We've got a problem," she whispered, giving his earlobe a nip to keep their cover. "Move with me." She guided their bodies around as she kept tight to him, never losing the beat.

He flicked his glance to the upper tier of the club, where men with guns were fanning out, their eyes searching the crowded dance floor. "We're blown," he said into her neck, his lips trailing against her soft skin. "They're looking for us. But Volkhov is up there."

"Big guy, receding hairline, mole under his left eye?" she asked, her voice cool.

"That's him." Their target, known in the mob world as the Wolf, was peering over the balcony railing. Volkhov ran an outfit of executioners and henchmen used by the top underworld organizations for protection and was notoriously difficult to photograph. All they needed to get from him was verification of identity. Nailing him would shut down some international violence and slow the spread of Russian mob power.

Three days earlier, Anderson had had a meeting with Volkhov, pretending to be a potential client for the executioner's services. The way the gunmen were searching the crowd indicated Volkhov had made the connection that Anderson was watching him. Since Volkhov was the suspicious type, with a network of informants, he probably knew about Violet as well. They needed an escape plan, but not before Anderson got the picture he wanted.

Anderson captured an image of Volkhov with his phone before dropping his head against her shoulder again. He needed to keep his face out of sight. "Hop up and let me carry you," he said. She did what he asked, wrapping her arms and legs tight around him. His hands molded to her butt, holding her in place.

"I got it," she said when he kissed her neck again. "Keep your head down. I can see the exit."

While keeping up the pretense of making out, she whispered directions in his ear and they worked their way across the dance floor. He trusted her quick, analytical brain to make the right calls and didn't hesitate to follow her instructions.

"Almost there," she breathed, her mouth against his temple. "Two steps to the right, and straight toward the emergency exit. Things are about to get ugly."

"Stop," a voice yelled in Russian and then in English, loud enough to be heard over the pounding music. Anderson shoved open the steel exit door, dumping them into an alley. Not a minute too soon. The sound of gunfire and echoes of screams came from the club, but Anderson was already running, still carrying Violet, not wanting to slow down long enough to put her on her feet. Down the block, a motorcycle idled at the curb, its driver a few steps away, handing a delivery to a woman in the entryway of an apartment building.

"Bike," he said as they approached, letting Violet slide down his body until her feet were on the pavement. Despite the urgent situation, the friction sent a zing through him—but they needed to move. He swung his leg over the motorcycle, and she climbed on behind him.

"Go," she yelled as the delivery driver lurched toward them with a cry. Her arms closed around him and her body pressed up against his.

He revved the bike, rocketing them away from the club and danger. With their cover blown, he couldn't risk returning to their apartment, so he headed for a nearby safe house. He wound them through the complex pattern of Moscow's streets, slowing the bike once it was clear they'd eluded immediate pursuit—from the mobsters as well as the motorcycle's rightful driver—and navigating carefully through a quiet residential area, not wanting to attract any attention as they approached the safe house and pulled into its parking garage.

They didn't speak as they rode the elevator to the fifth floor and he keyed in the security code he'd memorized before deploying on this mission. The door opened, and he pulled her inside before securing the lock and reactivating the alarm system.

"Did you get it?" she asked, her first words since they'd escaped.

"You bet," he answered. He took his phone from his pocket and showed her the image of the executioner. His face was clear and large on the screen. A second image showed him next to a known mob boss and directing the gunman in the club.

"Fantastic." She smiled, and Anderson's heart rate shot up. He should have thought better of his next move, but his body was still pumping with adrenaline. He yanked her to him for a victory kiss.

Her mouth opened to him, and he plunged his tongue in as he shoved her against the wall, hands roaming down her body, hips grinding against hers. Immediately he knew he didn't want to stop with a kiss. Weeks of sexual frustration burned through him, and he couldn't get enough of her. The attraction between them had almost throbbed at times, but they'd both backed away from acting on it. Until then. She pulled his shirt from his pants and slipped her hands underneath. Demanding fingers roamed over his stomach and rubbed across his nipples. She was driving him wild, and all he could feel was need.

"I want you," he said, not giving a damn that their relationship was supposed to be professional—or that they didn't always like each other.

"One thing we agree on." Her hands dropped lower and cupped his erection through his pants, making him moan.

Before she could do more, he hiked her dress up, taking it over her head when she lifted her arms. She wore only a lace thong underneath. He sucked in a breath. God, she was beautiful, even more than he'd imagined she'd be. He palmed her breasts before taking one nipple in his mouth.

"God, that's amazing," she murmured, arching into him as he sucked. Their lower bodies rubbed together while her hands continued to explore him, stroking long paths down his back to his butt. When she pulled his wallet from his pants pocket, he lifted his head to meet her eyes. She gave him a sultry smile. "Condom in here, right?"

"Good guess," he said, switching his attention to her other breast as his fingers traveled down her sides.

"It's what I do. Make guesses based on evidence"—she gasped when he squeezed her ass—"and observations. My assessment of you is that you're a condom-in-the-wallet kind of guy. Do you mind if I retrieve it?"

"Help yourself." A second later, he heard his wallet hit the floor behind him and took the condom from her. He removed his shirt while she undid his pants. With one motion, she hooked her fingers in the waistband of both trousers and boxers and shoved them down until he could step free. Only one wisp of fabric remained between them. He kissed her lips, scraping his tongue across hers, before moving his mouth down her neck, taking nips at her skin. He followed the valley between her breasts, down over her navel, and to the edge of the lace.

Her hands sank into his hair as he swirled his tongue over the fabric, tracing the outline of her cunt.

"Take them off," she breathed, but rather than wait for him, she pushed the panties down herself. He helped work the thong down her legs, touching and teasing as he went. "Take me against this wall." She was demanding as always, but he was willing to comply this once.

He stood and rolled the condom onto his dick. "Hop on."

She put her arms around his neck, making it easy for him to lift her. Her legs squeezed around him as they had in the club, but now there was nothing between them. He plunged into her, bracing her against the wall. She tipped her head back, giving him easy access to her throat and breasts.

Passion like he'd never known swamped him. He had to try to harness it or he'd come too quickly. He tried to slow the pace, but she squeezed her inner muscles around his dick, driving him on. They were both panting as their bodies pounded together. He didn't think he could last another minute when she came, a rough scream coming from her lips. He thrust into her one more time, and the orgasm took him in wave after wave of pleasure.

3

———————

"Where are we going?" Violet asked after sitting silently in the car for ten minutes. Fortunately, Nate had zonked as soon as they started moving. Car rides had that effect on him, even ones that changed roads and doubled back like this one was doing. Standard practice, she told herself. Anderson was taking evasive action. She'd used her own training to do the same thing in the past weeks when she felt she was being watched.

"No idea. Working on it." He spoke in choppy sentences, eyes flicking between the mirrors.

She sighed. They'd never been good at conversation. Intelligence work and sex were their joint areas of expertise. And they'd only done the second of those things once. But once had been enough. She twisted in her seat so she could catch Nate's profile. His head was resting against the padded side of the seat, not far from the bullet hole she'd seen earlier. She squeezed her eyes shut, fighting against the image that rose in her mind.

"Something behind us?" Anderson asked. "I don't see that black SUV in my mirror."

Had he forgotten about his son already?

"Nothing that shouldn't be there." She faced forward again, unwilling to engage about Nate and Anderson's role in his upbringing while they were fleeing for their lives. She had to think, kick her analyst brain into gear. The other incidents she'd described to Anderson had happened more than two weeks ago, and she'd begun to feel safe. What had made her assailant escalate from some creepy behaviors to riddling her car with bullets?

She had to look for the source of the change. Her eyes moved to Anderson's profile. The high forehead, long nose, surprisingly sensuous lips. She remembered what those felt like on her body and nearly shivered with desire. This was no time to be thinking about that night in Russia when they'd torn each other's clothes off and had primal sex against a wall.

The aftermath of that experience was more indicative of their relation-ship. They'd caught their breath and immediately turned away from each other. No postsex cuddling. No soft words. They'd each picked up their clothes and gone in opposite directions in the safe house. From then until they parted in Germany a day later, they'd only communicated when necessary.

One magical moment in Russia had produced the little guy behind her. She pulled the note from the outside pocket of the diaper bag where she'd stashed it and looked at it again. Rereading the Russian writing sent a chill down her spine. She wasn't scared for her own life, but if anything happened to Nate…

She flipped the paper over, looking for any clues that might identify the sender.

"Find anything?" Anderson asked as he merged onto a highway.

"Nothing that I can see." The fancy equipment at the lab where she worked might reveal more, but she didn't have access to that. And they'd both contaminated any evidence by handling the paper. "I'm thinking it can't be a coincidence that the attack was today. You arrived home from your deployment two days ago, and this was the first time we saw each other. Someone's been watching me and waiting to send us a message when we're together."

"Maybe," he conceded, "but we've never been a couple."

"We looked like one, though." That had been their cover story in Moscow. He played the role of a wealthy American who might be interested in making an arrangement with the Russian mob, and she'd been his eye candy. The truth couldn't have been more different. Her analysis work had made her the primary on their mission, and he'd been support and protection. Since they both viewed themselves as being in charge, they'd disagreed nearly daily. Some of that was just the tension of the mission, some was the latent desire between them. "And... I don't know. Even if our cover is partly or completely blown, maybe my pregnancy convinced them our relationship was real."

Anderson remained silent for several minutes. "If you're right about this, we need to change cars. They probably have intel on me, including what I drive."

"That would be a start," she said, "but we need a safe place to go so we can figure this out. We can't drive forever." Safe houses existed, both government and private ones, but she didn't have access to that list. Her supervisor would, but she wondered if that would be a smart move. Protocol told her she should report this incident and wait for directions, but her instincts, which were rarely wrong, told her otherwise.

"Are you still thinking of calling in?" he asked, exiting the highway and taking a road that ran perpendicular to it. She realized they were slowly working their way southwest from his house.

"I don't think that's wise. Combined with what happened today, the breach concerns me." She ticked over the details of the breach, the ones she knew. Were there more?

"Should have been sealed," he said.

"In a neat and tidy world, it would have been," she said. Anderson was used to the closed ranks of SEAL teams, where nothing dangerous was allowed to simmer. Her world was much more nebulous. Sometimes threats were permitted to exist, even encouraged, to see where they were going and who they tracked back to. She'd advised taking that course of action herself in the past in certain situations. It all felt different when it was targeted at her.

She'd thought from the beginning that there was a high probability the breach was the work of the Wolf's organization. Like their leader, they were relentless hunters. Volkhov himself was supposedly being held in a Russian prison, but that didn't mean his pack was lying around licking their wounds. Or that he was unable to give directions

"This all feels too volatile to me," she finally said.

"No kidding," he muttered.

She swung her gaze to him. "What I'm saying is that I need time to analyze and assess. You write stuff in your little notepads." She reached across and tapped the pad of paper he always carried in his chest pocket. "I have to let intel coalesce in my brain."

"It helps me to write it down," he said, looking annoyed.

"I get that. You'd be scribbling away right now if you weren't driving." It surprised her how much she knew about him and his methods. They'd been together just six weeks in Russia, but she'd had plenty of opportunity to observe him during that time.

"You're right," he admitted with a hint of reluctance. "I've seen you think your way out of some tough spots. I learned to trust that about you."

She was mildly surprised he'd acknowledged her expertise, but before she could reply, Nate whimpered in his seat, making her turn. The baby was rolling his head from side to side. After a minute, he stuck his thumb in his mouth and drifted back to sleep. That was a habit she'd have to help him break later, but for the moment she was grateful it settled him.

"He's okay," she said, even though Anderson hadn't asked. Her relief was short lived when she faced forward again. Anderson had gone rigid next to her. What was that about? She checked her side mirror, looking for signs of trouble, but they were on a country road without another car in sight. "What is it?"

A muscle in his jaw twitched. "We've got things to discuss… about him."

So that was it. Her hiding Nate's existence must have seemed like the ultimate betrayal. Still, she'd had her reasons. Good ones, she still believed. None of that helped her current situation, though. She rarely cracked under pressure—professional pressure, anyway. Since having a child, she'd found her personal world had shifted. She felt things more and more deeply.

At the moment she felt a wave of nerves, almost enough to make her squirm. "Okay. If we're going to get through… whatever is going on" —she gestured, encompassing the car, their situation—"we need to trust each other, which means you have to believe I'm telling you the truth about Nate. So, do you believe he's yours?" It pained her to have to ask, but it would be a reasonable concern on his part. She could tell him that she hadn't slept with anyone else for almost a year before Nate was conceived and no one since, but she couldn't prove it.

"He's mine," Anderson said with almost no inflection. "I can see it in his face."

She almost chuckled at the way he said it. She'd read an article in *Scientific American* disputing the theory that first-born children resembled their fathers as a kind of evolutionary guarantee the father would accept the child. Supposedly, it wasn't true, but she wondered about that, because she certainly saw Anderson when she looked at their son.

"Good to hear," she said. "And I told you why I didn't contact you before you deployed."

"Yeah." He sounded skeptical, which didn't surprise her. It was probably hard for him to believe that she'd been halfway through her pregnancy before acknowledging it to herself. "What about after you realized you were pregnant—and after Nate's birth? Did you even attempt to reach me?"

"No, I didn't," she admitted. She could have gotten word to him if she'd wanted to. She knew the channels and how to cut through the red tape. That ability had allowed her to pinpoint the day Anderson arrived home from his deployment, but she hadn't used it to locate him earlier.

"You see my problem, then," he said. "You withheld information. Never trust a source that does that." It was a standard in intelligence work where sources sometimes played for both sides. They were compromised and deemed untrustworthy. You might listen to what they had to say, but you didn't trust it.

"I did a risk analysis. Actually, I did several." She'd reevaluated her situation every month. Each time she'd concluded that Anderson didn't need to know about Nate. Her most recent analysis, though, had led to a different outcome. The data hadn't changed, but her perspective had. If someone had kept a child as beautiful and sweet as

Nate from her, she'd have been ready to do murder. She'd had no way of knowing whether Anderson would care even a little bit, but it was his decision to make. She couldn't do it for him.

The unknown in her prediction had been Anderson's reaction to being a father. She had no hard data to indicate what his response would be, but her gut had told her he wouldn't accept fatherhood easily. Considering the circumstances, she felt no joy in being right about that.

"And what were your findings?" he prompted.

"As you know—since I'm here—I recently decided you deserved to know." She couldn't elaborate on that. It was an assumption built on emotion, not fact, and she wasn't sure he'd understand. Sometimes she didn't understand it herself, but there it was.

Their situation, though… Even the best data wouldn't have pointed to her being on the run with a baby and the baby's father, who might not want to have anything to do with her or Nate. She blew out a sigh, frustrated at the lack of a plan that would guide them. She didn't have enough information and no resources she was willing to tap. They could drive to Hilton Head Island, where her mother now lived, but she wasn't taking trouble to her mom's door. She'd dismissed that as a possibility an hour ago.

"We need to find a place to spend the night," she said after a long silence. Nate would wake up and not like being confined to his car seat. Plus, she needed to feed him.

"I'm on it." Anderson tapped a button on his steering wheel, seemingly relieved to have something to do. "Call Patrick." He spoke the command and waited while the automated system dialed.

"Hey, Anderson," a man's voice answered on the second ring. "Glad you're back in the States. Do you want to come over and see—"

"Sorry, man. Not today. I've got a problem," Anderson said, then efficiently explained about the attack on Violet's car, the note, and the baby in the back seat.

"You've got a kid?" whoever this Patrick was interrupted to ask. The bullets in her car and the note in Russian didn't give him pause, but the idea of Anderson as a father made him react. That was interesting but not comforting.

"Yeah, he's just a baby," Anderson said with no warmth in his tone.

"Let me get this straight," Patrick said. "You're on the run with a baby. Man, I thought *my* life was complicated. What do you need from me?"

"A safe place to land for the night and a different car," Anderson said. His eyes had never left the road or the mirrors. "You got any connections I can use?"

"Maybe. Let me make some phone calls. Kenton might have some ideas, too. Does he know about your kid?"

"Negative. I found out today," Anderson said. "Call me back when you have something." He clicked the button to end the call.

Violet had heard frustration in his voice, but she couldn't be sure of the source. Was it being a father or their situation that was breaking his cool?

She hoped it was the second. Nate wasn't a problem. He was a child, a beautiful, lovable little boy. Her mother's heart broke to think Anderson might view their son as nothing more than an inconvenience. Of course Nate made things more complicated and brought her world a degree of fear that bordered on terror given their circumstances, but when she snuggled her child against her, any trouble was worth it.

Would Anderson come to feel that, as she had? Or was he planning to walk away as soon as he could? She'd be okay if he did. Disappointed and sad for Nate, but okay. As she'd told Anderson at his house, she didn't need anything from him. Her father had been out of the picture by the time she was one, and her mother had been amazing. She made single motherhood look easy. Not once had Violet felt deprived. She'd been curious about her father, but she'd never longed for one because she knew she had everything she needed in her mother.

Violet could follow her mother's example and be the same kind of parent, giving her baby mountains of love and security in other ways. She was willing to raise Nate that way, but would her child be even better off if he had two loving parents? She thought so.

Violet drummed her fingers against her leg, wishing she had the missing pieces to the puzzle they were in… and access to Anderson's thoughts. No hope of either seemed imminent. At the moment, she'd settle for getting out of the car.

They kept driving, with Anderson periodically taking calls from Patrick and Kenton. The other men appeared to be close friends as well as SEAL teammates. Between the two of them, they set up an exchange of cars and a hotel they deemed safe for the night. It was a temporary fix to a problem that had no foreseeable end.

4

———

"Is he sick?" Anderson asked when they were safely in the hotel room. They'd been on the road for five hours, and Nate had cried for the last one. Driving with a crying kid in the back seat should be some special endorsement on your license or used in training people to overcome distractions, because it had been hard as hell to keep his focus.

"I don't think so. Babies are sensitive to changes in routine. Today's been rough." Violet had made a makeshift changing table on top of the desk in the room. She seemed to have quite the supply of stuff in that one bag. A padded mat, extra clothes, diapers, wipes… and she'd used them all in the past half hour.

"Never seen so much poop," Anderson commented as Violet bagged another messy diaper in plastic. "You sure he's okay?"

"Look, I'm not a pediatrician," she snapped. "I do have five months of experience as a parent, though, and you've had one day. Just let me do my thing."

Anderson held his hands up and backed off. That tone of voice was much more what he was used to from her. She didn't like having her competence questioned. And, hell, in this case she definitely was the expert in the room. Anderson sat on the edge of the bed and looked at Nate, who was gurgling peacefully now, nothing like the screaming kid from the car or the pooping machine he'd been since they got in the room. Was that kind of rapid change common with kids?

Violet had one hand on Nate's stomach while she dug deeper into the bag with her other one. Should he offer to help her? She seemed like she was managing, but he didn't like to feel useless.

"Do you want me to find a store and get some… baby stuff?" he asked.

She huffed out a sigh. "I suppose."

"Okay," he said, pulling the notepad from his pocket and flipping to a blank page. "Tell me what to get."

"A few packs of diapers, size two," she said.

"They have sizes?" he asked. She answered with a glare. "Got it. What else?"

"Wipes. A couple of outfits. Get ones labeled either six months or six to nine months."

He scribbled her request, not pointing out that the baby was five months old. There must be a mystery to this he didn't understand, or else his kid was big for his age. Anderson liked that idea better. "Anything else?"

"No, that should get us by." Her voice cracked, making him wonder how close she was to tears. She always seemed so able to handle anything, but apparently today had her on edge.

"I'll be back as soon as I can," he said and left the room.

A quick search on his phone directed Anderson to a nearby Target, where he made his way to the baby section. Diapers first. He sucked in a breath at the wall of choices. Was a size two the same in all the brands? He started reading labels. It seemed so, but what did he know? He selected a couple of different packages and got extra wipes as well before heading to the clothing section.

Buying baby clothes was not something Anderson had ever expected to do, but he sorted through a rack of tiny outfits until he found one in primary colors and another with sailboats on the front. That was a start. He'd have to get Nate a US Navy T-shirt. He'd seen those on the kids of his fellow SEALs.

Wait. What the hell was he thinking? It wasn't like he planned to help raise the boy. Which was probably what Violet expected. He could guess her analysis had showed he'd be a poor father. She hadn't admitted that to him in the car, but he could tell she doubted him.

He'd be angry about that if he didn't feel so damn worried about their situation being complicated by having a baby with them. Kids made everything tougher. He'd seen that over and over with his SEAL teammates—including Patrick, who'd had to fight for custody of his daughter. Not a place Anderson had ever wanted to go. Life was easier if he only had to worry about himself—he'd been managing that since he was ten. That he could do successfully, but adding a baby and a woman to the mix blew his carefully planned life all to hell.

He gave himself a shake. He'd figure all that out later. First, he had to deal with the threat against Violet and Nate. He passed the food section his way to the checkout and detoured to pick up a couple of premade sandwiches and a few pieces of fruit. He looked at the cart, then grabbed a package of chocolate cookies for Violet and some protein bars for himself.

When he returned to the hotel, Nate was fussing again.

"Thank goodness," Violet said in greeting. "More diapers." As she brushed her hair back from her face, her gaze fell on the food. "Good call."

"Do you want me to open any of this up?" he offered, happy that he'd pleased her.

"Later." She boosted Nate onto her shoulder and paced with him around the small room. "Come on, little man, give Mama a break, okay?" Her voice was soft and soothing, and it seemed to be having an effect. Nate's eyes started to close.

Not wanting to disturb either of them, Anderson slipped out to check the area around the hotel. He walked around the parking lot and a three-block radius, looking for black SUVs—though, of course, the assailants could have changed vehicles. Still, nothing he saw raised any red flags. As he headed back, he phoned Patrick for an update.

"I think you should call Rogers," Patrick suggested. "He's got civilian connections that we don't."

"Good idea," Anderson said. He'd have thought of contacting Dan Rogers, a former SEAL who now owned a private security company, himself if the day hadn't been such a shitshow. "I'll do that. Thanks for your help."

"No problem. Hey, Anderson, what's your son's name?"

"Nate." He didn't elaborate because he was still trying to process the fact that twenty-four hours ago he hadn't even known of the baby's existence.

"Take care of him," Patrick said. "'Night."

Anderson made his way back to the hotel room and paused outside the door to listen. Silence. He went in. Violet held her finger to her lips and pointed to the sleeping baby in the center of the bed.

"I've been waiting for you to come back," she whispered. "Can you keep an eye on him while I take a bath?"

"Yeah, I guess. What do I do if he wakes up and cries?" Anderson shot the snoozing baby a look. He seemed to be out, but looks were deceiving when it came to kids. He'd learned that today.

"Hold him. I need twenty minutes to myself, okay?" She looked more tired than he'd ever seen her. "Can you give me that?"

He nodded and caught her arm when she went to turn away. "Did you call anyone while I was out?"

"No. I think it's best not to. I need time and more information to analyze the threat. I'm not comfortable with turning this over to the agency." Her voice sounded determined, but he caught an edge of fear. "We're better off on our own for a while."

"Suits me." Anderson could have reached out to his commanding officer for assistance, but like her, he was reluctant to involve others until they had more facts. Rogers, whom he'd known for years and who was no longer part of the military hierarchy, was the one person he was confident he could trust. He took a minute to tell her about the former SEAL and his company.

"If you're that confident of his integrity, he seems like our best bet," she agreed. "His firm can gather intel for me to analyze."

"And what am I supposed to do while you're doing that?" Anderson asked.

"Same as always," she said with a wan smile. "Keep us safe. Yell if you need me."

She disappeared into the bathroom, and he heard water running in the tub a minute later. He turned the lights low and checked outside the window for any problems before pulling the drapes shut tight. There was nothing else he could do, so he sat and took out his notebook. He unwrapped the remaining sandwich—Violet must have eaten the other one while he was out—and quickly ate it while he began writing down everything from the day, along with pertinent information from their mission in Moscow.

He'd been at work for only a few minutes when Nate stirred, his little fists shooting into the air. A second later, he began to whimper. Anderson rushed over and found the boy's eyes wide open and staring.

"I need you to sleep, buddy," he murmured. "Your mom's tired and needs a break. And I've got no idea what to do with you." The whimper became a sob, and Nate's face turned red and scrunched as if he was getting ready to really yell. "Come on. Don't do that. Here, I'll pick you up, okay?"

Anderson slipped his arms under the boy and brought him to his shoulder. He'd held him a couple of times during the day, but never when he was crying or couldn't be readily handed back to Violet.

"How can someone so little make so much trouble?" Anderson muttered. His son's weight felt like nothing in his arms, but he still worried that he wasn't doing this right. He rubbed Nate's back like he'd seen Violet do and put a little bounce in his step as he paced across the room.

"You like that. What else makes you happy?" Anderson looked down at the boy's face. He was studying Anderson as if waiting for some-thing. "You want me to talk?" He kept his tone gentle. "I can do that. I'm guessing you have no idea what I'm saying, so this conversation is totally off the record, right?"

Nate gurgled and stuck his thumb in his mouth. The kid was cute, but Jesus, Anderson wasn't ready for this. He had too much baggage of his own. Since he didn't know what to say, he spilled out what was on his mind.

"My daddy was a jerk, you know." Anderson would have used a stronger word if he'd been talking to an adult. "The worst kind of man. Irresponsible, criminal, abusive when it suited him. I've spent my life trying to be different from him. You see, my dad had a kid he didn't want. Me. My birth did nothing but cause problems for my parents. You've got it better than that. Your mama loves you, and you're lucky there. You aren't so lucky in a daddy, though. And I've gotta tell you that I didn't ask for this—for you." He paused, feeling guilty about his words, but that guilt wasn't stronger than the fear inside him. "You seem nice when you aren't screaming, but there's no place in my life for a baby. I'm just not cut out for that kind of life. I've got friends, teammates, people I trust, but I never let anyone close. You know why?" The baby looked up at him with big eyes. "I'll tell you. Here's my fatherly advice, probably the only bit I'll ever give you. If you let people close, they mess with you. Mess with your head, and you've got to dig your way out of that. Pull yourself up from nothing. It's hard, but I did it."

Anderson was silent for a minute until Nate stirred again, rubbing his head against Anderson's shoulder. "Still want to talk? Let me make my point again. I was never meant to be a daddy. I'm sorry, but that's the truth. I can't care for you. It would be… it would be too much. I hope you can understand that."

He turned and almost collided with Violet. She was wrapped in a robe, and her eyes blazed. "How much did you hear?" he asked, not that he regretted his words. They were the truth. No one should trust him to raise a child, because he didn't trust himself to do that.

"Enough." She took Nate from him and cuddled him into her body. "I was wondering what would have happened today if my car hadn't been riddled with bullets. I guess I have my answer."

"Violet," he started, but she waved him off.

"It's fine. As I told you, I don't need you—and neither does Nate. I can manage as a single parent. As a matter of fact, I don't need you now. Just help me get to a safe house, and I'll take it from there." Her tone was brusque, businesslike.

"I'm going to see this mess through," he said. He'd never wanted children or a relationship, but he'd make sure no harm came to Nate and Violet. Since he was already neck deep in this situation, he'd do his best to protect them. After it ended was a different story.

"Not necessary." She eyed him over Nate's head. "Now, I'm tired and I want to go to sleep. Nate and I will take the bed. I assume the floor works for you."

He nodded, not knowing what else to say, since he wasn't going to apologize for speaking the truth. Maybe it was just as well she'd overheard him. It got his position out in the open.

5

———————

Violet rolled over in the still-dark hotel room and listened to Nate's steady breathing. All the child-rearing books said not to have a baby in bed with you, and she could see why that was. She'd been so worried about accidentally hurting him in the night that she'd hardly slept.

He'd woken once to be fed, but other than that he'd been peaceful. Unlike her. She hated where she'd left things with Anderson. But she wasn't surprised. She had hoped he'd welcome fatherhood, but she hadn't expected him to. Not really. She'd let hope color her assessment, but in her heart, she'd known the truth. She'd been right about him. Good for her. But it didn't make her feel the least bit vindicated or happy.

She'd thought, not very rationally, that Anderson would meet Nate and something would click, an instant bond would form between father and son. She'd felt the connection to her child the second she saw a positive symbol on the pregnancy test. And when she'd seen the image of his face at her first ultrasound, she'd fallen in love. Not that she hadn't been frightened at the prospect of having a baby. She had been, but she'd also wanted the child.

None of that was there for Anderson, and she couldn't force it. He'd fathered Nate. At least he hadn't denied that, but he couldn't love his son. God, that made her sad.

She pushed herself up so her back rested against the headboard. The bedside clock read six. A lamp on the other side of the room clicked on low, and Anderson stood. She wasn't surprised that he was awake. He seemed to always be on alert. That quality must come with his job. Their eyes met across the room.

"Sorry about last night," she said in a low voice. "I didn't mean to snap at you for being honest about your feelings for Nate."

"It's not that I don't care what happens to him. It's just that..." He walked closer. "I'll help you out financially. The Navy will set it up. I know they do for other guys. They'll direct deposit part of my pay to your account. And if you ever need anything else, just let me know."

Violet felt annoyance at his offer of child support. Did he think that was her motivation for involving him? Even in part? "I don't want your money," she said. "My income is plenty to take care of Nate and me." As an analyst, her salary was likely higher than Anderson's. If she switched to the private sector, she could easily double her annual income. Money wasn't the issue.

"Still, it's the decent thing to do," he mumbled, looking down at her.

She wanted to argue that decent would be giving her emotional support and loving their son. Money had nothing to do with decency in this situation. But Anderson seemed incapable of understanding that. When she'd first been partnered with him, she'd done some digging about his background. She knew he was an only child with no relationship with his parents. Their backgrounds were murky; the only records she'd found were criminal. So she wasn't surprised that he had no sense of family… but it still hurt her.

"Please. Don't bother. Really," she said, swinging her legs to the floor. "I'm going to get moving. If you could take me to where this car is waiting, I'll go on from there solo."

"Not a good idea." His tone, which had seemed uncertain, was suddenly firm. "I put some things in motion during the night."

"With Rogers?" she asked.

"He's got a place for us to stay," Anderson said. "It's in Tennessee. It'll take us the better part of the day to drive there, but it's a house in a quiet suburb where we can go… unnoticed."

In other words, they'd look like a young couple with a baby, which wouldn't attract attention. All appearances would point to them being a family.

"Does he have temporary identities for us, too?" None of this would work if they were using their real names and credit cards.

"He's working on it," Anderson said with a glance at Nate, who was starting to wiggle.

"Rogers must be a good friend," she commented as she reached for Nate and lifted him into her lap. He was still warm and cuddly from sleep. She loved mornings with him.

"Being a SEAL is a brotherhood," Anderson said. He watched their son but made no attempt to reach for him.

His comment, though, made it clear that Anderson did understand family. He'd forged those bonds with his fellow SEALs. Why wouldn't he take the time to build one with his own son? It mystified her, but she couldn't get upset about it. Not again.

"I'm thankful he's willing to help," she said. "I thought about it more overnight. The pieces of this puzzle don't click together. Too much is missing, and I'm not feeling like I can trust the agency to assist us."

"Go with your gut," Anderson said. "It's usually right. We should get moving."

Three hours later, Violet was ready to tear her hair out. Anderson kept hitting the preset buttons on his car stereo, sending them on a chaotic journey between classic rock, country, and reggae. She'd known he was a complicated man, but his music choices made her look for a stronger descriptor. He never settled on one style for long, and they seemed at odds with each other. Was that a reflection of his internal self?

When he hit a button that took them to contemporary jazz, she couldn't stay silent any longer. "Any chance I can command the radio?" she asked, trying for a joking tone.

He shook his head. "Driver's choice. That's the rule."

"Whose rule?" she asked.

He glanced at her, surprise on his face. "The rule of all road trips."

Her experience with road trip music was somewhat different. If she traveled with her mom, it was Broadway hits. With girlfriends, pop music pumped from the stereo. Both of those choices were mutual, not dictatorial. Lately, she'd been listening to music meant to enhance child development, but Nate wasn't picky. He seemed to like anything. He'd babbled along in the back seat through Anderson's changes in genre.

"I'm not familiar with that rule. But if that's how it works, I'd be happy to drive for a while," she said, certain that he'd say no. In her experience, men liked to stay in control of the wheel.

"Sure," he said and pulled off at the next rest area.

Before she started driving, she flipped through the options on the radio and found one dedicated to pop music from the past ten years. Perfect. She liked it, though she figured Anderson wouldn't. She merged back into traffic as the music played. The familiar songs were good background for her thoughts and a way to sort through the chaos of the past day. So much had happened since she'd waited nervously on Anderson's doorstep with Nate in her arms to tell him that he had a son.

Here they were on the run together in uncomfortable silence. If they were going to masquerade as a family, some of the tension had to go. They were both good actors when it came to espionage, but she couldn't live on edge for however long it took to resolve this. She needed to bridge the gap between them, at least temporarily, so they could work as a team again.

She glanced over at him. He was tapping along to the rhythm of Nickelback's "Gotta Be Somebody." Pretty soon, she heard him joining in on the chorus. What the heck—she knew the lyrics, too. They sang the refrain together.

He gave her a glance and an unexpected grin when she danced in her seat and kept the rhythm with her fingertips on the steering wheel. This was fun, almost like a real road trip. They joined voices on the next verse.

She'd never thought much about the meaning of the song, just enjoyed the beat and the video as a teenager, but now she wondered if the words about how there was a person for everyone out there held some truth that she'd missed at sixteen. The lead vocalist sang the final lines, and a moment later a different song began.

"I've always liked that one," Anderson said.

"Me, too," she agreed. "It reminds me of being in high school."

"Is that a good memory?"

"Some of it." They hadn't been the greatest days of her life, but overall the experience had been good. "My friends and I had a lot of fun."

"I'll bet you were a serious student," he said.

"Had to be." She'd taken all the advanced classes her school offered. "My mom expected nothing less, but she also got that I was a kid and wanted to enjoy a carefree life while I could. I think… I think she understood that more than most parents, since she raised me by herself."

"Has to be hard," he commented, "being a single mom."

"I've only had a taste of it, but there have been times when it would have been nice to be able to hand Nate off to someone." A few late nights stuck out in her head, times she'd paced the floor with the baby for hours and couldn't get him to settle. "He was colicky at two months."

"Colicky?" Anderson questioned the unfamiliar word.

"Yeah, no one knows what causes it, exactly"—she'd done enough research to confirm that—"but some babies just cry and cry and cry, and you can't soothe them. That was a rough few weeks. I'm not complaining, though. I wouldn't trade him for anything."

"Nate has someone to love him and have his life in their hands, like the song says. That's good." Anderson's voice had turned serious.

"I don't think the lyrics refer to moms and babies. The song's about finding the right person to love and trust." She'd never worried about that much, never obsessed about a guy the way her friends had. Maybe it was her upbringing, but she'd never imagined the big moment of finding true love, marrying, and following the path of kids and carpools. Instead, she'd focused on college and career. Guys were a nice distraction when she wanted a friend with benefits, but she'd never taken any of them seriously.

"The song could be applied to anyone," Anderson said with a shrug.

"Maybe. If that's the case, who is it for you?" she asked, not really sure of his reaction. Would he answer her or clam up? It was an interesting experiment. Did Anderson Park talk about his feelings? Had he ever wished someone was out there for him?

The pause was long as Lady Gaga sang and Nate gurgled in the back seat. Violet let the silence extend. If Anderson chose not to respond, she'd leave it alone.

"I had two good friends in high school," he said finally. "Patrick and Kenton. In a lot of ways, we were nothing alike. Different backgrounds. But we stuck together—played football and ran track. After graduation, they both went to the Naval Academy, and I enlisted by the usual route."

"I thought you went to Monterey," she said. All branches of the military used the Department of Defense's language institute to train language experts. Anderson spoke multiple languages, a skill that had gotten them placed together in Russia.

"I did," he said. "I got sent there after basic. I learned Russian first and then stayed on for Arabic."

She wanted to laugh. He said it casually, but the intensive immersive language program was anything but casual. The fact that he'd studied two languages there was almost unheard of.

"So you stayed friends with these guys?" she prompted, hoping to keep him talking.

"Yeah, we managed to get in the same SEAL class. Did our training together."

"But you weren't on the same team?" It was unusual for three guys who knew each other to be placed together on those teams. She'd worked with enough Special Forces units to be aware of that.

"We are," he said, surprising her, "but occasionally one of us gets shifted around, like when we were in Russia. And then Patrick took a leave to deal with family issues. I'm looking forward to serving with them again soon."

"So they're your somebody?" she concluded.

"Yeah. I don't need anyone else." He sounded distracted, so she glanced at him. His eyes were focused on the side mirror.

"What is it?" she asked, suddenly aware of his tension.

"SUV behind us," he said.

"It's been back there for a couple miles." She'd seen it in her mirror, but since they were on a busy highway, she hadn't thought anything of it—and she'd been distracted by their conversation.

"The dent in the bumper. Maryland plates." He ticked off the details. "That's the vehicle that was outside my house yesterday."

"What?" She sat up straighter in her seat, her eyes shifting between the mirrors as often as she looked forward. The evasive driving training she'd received ran through her head. She'd employed some of that in recent weeks, but this was different. The stakes were higher now that these guys had taken aggressive action.

"We need to lose him," Anderson said. "Get off at the next exit. Just casually, like nothing's wrong."

She switched into the right lane and waited the mile until she could leave the highway. "What's your plan?" she asked, keeping her voice level.

"Just do what I ask," he said as they approached the end of the exit ramp. "Okay, gun it and get back on the highway."

She did what he said, punching the accelerator and merging back onto the highway. The black SUV that had followed her onto the exit had to wait for cross traffic, giving her a little time but—when it reappeared behind her—confirming that they were being followed.

"Go to the far-left lane," Anderson instructed, pivoting in his seat. "And keep it moving."

Their speed increased until it was twenty over the posted limit. The black SUV was trying to catch up. A truck swung into her lane just ahead of her, forcing her to brake.

"Pass on the right," Anderson said.

She squeezed in, cutting off another truck, and pushed the pedal to the floor.

"Good. Take the next exit. It's in a half mile. Maybe there'll be a gas station or fast food place we can pull into and be less visible for a few minutes."

She changed lanes again, saying a silent apology to the vehicles around her for her erratic driving. This time, when she exited, she blew the stop sign at the bottom of the ramp, took a sharp left, and pulled up under the bridge so the highway traffic couldn't see her as it passed overhead.

"Nice tactic," Anderson said. "You've done this before."

"I've had some training," she said, pleased with herself for staying calm.

"Yeah? I thought you were all about running the data."

"There's a practical side to what I do, too." The basic evasive techniques course had been mandatory for any agents who worked in the field, but she'd gone back for a more advanced one.

"You mean defensive," he said, his tone revealing admiration. "I think we lost them, but they won't be fooled for long." He tapped the navigation screen on his dashboard. "We need an alternate route, which is going to add time to our drive."

Hopefully it'll keep us safe, she added silently. She'd been in dangerous spots before, but having Nate with them changed how she reacted. She settled in to drive, following the new directions provided by the system, while Anderson made a phone call, presumably to Rogers. An hour later they transferred Nate and what little they had with them into an SUV crossover that was perfect for living in the suburbs before getting back on the road.

6

Anderson woke before more than a hint of light was in the sky. He could see a patch of gray out a window that faced into the backyard, but he was too damned tired to move yet. It had been past midnight when they'd arrived at the safe house and unloaded the car. Nate had alternately cried and slept for the last two hours of the journey, making that time seem twice as long. Finally, they'd made their way into a suburb of Nashville and to the safe house Rogers's company had located for them.

Fortunately, it came furnished, including a room set up for a baby. Anderson owed Rogers an enormous debt of gratitude, probably one too big to ever repay. After getting Nate in bed, Anderson and Violet had both collapsed on the couch and nearly fallen asleep leaning against each other. He'd insisted she take the only bedroom that was made up. He'd stayed on the couch, which was more comfortable than the floor he'd slept on the night before.

He'd just closed his eyes again, hoping to drift back to sleep, when the scrape of a shoe on concrete had everything in him going tense. Someone was outside the Cape Cod–style home. He'd done a circuit of the house in the dark the night before. His understanding of the property wasn't perfect, but his hearing had never been faulty.

Another whisper of sound and then low voices came from outside the front door. He grabbed the gun he'd kept handy during the night and silently rose from the couch to approach the door. A window of beveled glass bordered it. Keeping clear of that, he moved to where another window gave him a view of the front steps. He twitched back the curtains and saw two dark figures bent over in the pale morning light.

What the hell kind of a safe house was this? Was it already compromised?

He watched for another minute, but he couldn't see any weapons. Might as well confront this head-on.

He whipped open the front door and came face-to-face with two women who looked to be in their fifties. They stared at him, eyes wide, and he quickly assessed the threat. They wore fancy warm-up outfits and looked as though they were off to the tennis courts at the local country club. Not what he'd expected. He glanced behind them, fearing they were a front for something more nefarious, but he saw nothing to concern him.

"Oh… sorry," he said when one of the women dropped her gaze to the gun he held. He quickly stashed it on a shelf out of sight. Then he realized they were staring at his bare chest. He'd slept in only athletic shorts. Anderson wasn't tatted up like many of his fellow SEALs, but he had scars from injuries he'd sustained on missions. The women were staring at one that cut a jagged line down his torso. Not making the right kind of impression on the neighbors, he realized, if that's who these women were.

"Um… hi," the taller of the two women said, bringing her gaze up to his face. "I'm Evie Walker, and this is Kelly Sams. We thought you'd like some cinnamon buns."

Anderson glanced down to see a tray of pastries sitting on the steps. That explained the crouched figures, he guessed.

"And coffee," Kelly said, indicating the thermos. "We thought you probably didn't have time to unpack yet, since you arrived so late. I can never get going in the morning without a strong cup of coffee."

He stared at the women, trying to look unthreatening, but his senses were still on alert. These strangers seemed to know when he and Violet had arrived. Were they already being watched?

"I live just over there," Kelly said, pointing behind them, "and we were up late bingeing *The Crown* and drinking a bottle of wine when we saw you pull in. Here, it's in the note." She nervously thrust a piece of paper at Anderson. He flipped it open and scanned the words, which ended with, "Welcome to the neighborhood. Enjoy breakfast."

"Thanks," he said, trying to decide if these two were for real. This was a bit *Stepford Wives* for him. He glanced down the street, where lights were coming on in other houses. A couple of people were hitting the streets for early-morning exercise. It seemed like a normal place. Not that he'd ever lived in suburbia, but it looked just how suburbs were portrayed in the movies.

"We thought that there was nothing like a warm breakfast to ease a move," Evie said, retrieving the cinnamon rolls from the step. "Moving is so hard."

"My mother's recipe. I've never met anyone who didn't like it," Kelly added as she peeked around him, trying to see farther into the house. "This place has sat empty for almost six months. The last people moved out overnight, and we never heard what happened to them. We hope you and your family will be more a part of the community."

Anderson had no idea how to respond to that. Evie and Kelly were either great liars or unaware that the place was a safe house where all the residents were likely to be transient. And Anderson had no plans to join in community events, whatever those might be. He'd grown up in a mobile home. There'd been other trailers within ten feet, but it had never been a neighborhood. Even the city had viewed it as an eyesore, and shortly after Anderson left for basic training, some kind of rezoning had gone through that allowed them to move everyone out and build a condo complex on the site. He hadn't been the least bit sorry to see the place erased, but the reality was that—with that as his only background—he lacked the skills needed to react to neighborly overtures.

He should say something, but words failed him. He was opening his mouth to force out a *thank you* when he felt a warm hand on his back. Violet was up. He glanced at her, feeling overwhelming gratitude for her being there to greet the neighbors. She was smiling at the women as if she was delighted to meet them. With Nate curled into her side, his thumb stuck in his mouth, she looked the image of a carefree young mother.

"You should have come got me, honey. I didn't know we had company. Good morning," she said to Kelly and Evie as if she found strangers on her doorstep every day. "How sweet of you to bring us a treat. These smell delicious. And coffee, too. So thoughtful of you. I'm Violet, and this is my husband Anderson."

When they'd arrived late the night before, they'd found an envelope containing new identities and credit cards waiting for them on the dining room table. Rogers's firm had wisely kept their first names and altered the surnames, making it less likely that either of them would misspeak.

"And who is this little guy?" Kelly asked as Violet handed Nate to Anderson.

Anderson was happy that he was getting better at holding the boy. He'd lost the awkward sensation he'd had the first few times and was able to cuddle Nate to his chest in a way that he hoped looked natural.

"Aww…" Evie sighed, her eyes fixed on Nate and Anderson. "He's so precious."

"This is our son, Nate," Violet said. Her arm went around Anderson's waist, supporting the pretense that they were a happy couple.

"How old is he? Oh, he's just adorable," Kelly gushed, reaching out to tickle the baby's feet.

"Five months," Violet answered with a smile.

When Evie tried to stroke Nate's cheek, Anderson instinctively took a half step back. The women probably meant no harm, but they were still unknown. And he protected what was his.

How had Nate suddenly been put in that category? Anderson pulled his attention back to the conversation. He couldn't afford to get distracted.

"He's getting to that age where he's nervous around strangers," Violet was explaining, "and we don't want to upset him today. Yesterday was…" She left the sentence unfinished, allowing the women to fill in the details.

"Oh, yes, moving is so hard on everyone, especially babies," Kelly said immediately. "We understand. Welcome to the neighborhood."

"Thank you." Violet smiled at them. "I'm sure in a few days, when we're settled in, Nate'll be ready for company." She took the coffee and cinnamon rolls from them and said goodbye.

"Unexpected," Anderson commented as soon as he'd closed the door.

"Yes," Violet agreed. "It's not even seven in the morning. What kind of neighborhood is this?"

"I don't know, but you bought us at least a few days' peace. Good thinking, using Nate as an excuse."

Violet flashed him a smile that made him remember why he'd been so attracted to her in Moscow. "One of the perks of parenthood. A baby can always be used to get out of sticky situations."

"Let's hope that continues to be true," he said, following her through the house to the kitchen, still feeling unsettled about the visit. He wasn't used to people being friendly and welcoming. Maybe they were harmless, but it worried him. "I'm going to take a look at the house's defenses." They'd entered by using a pass code Rogers had texted to him, but that didn't seem like enough of a barrier.

"Does something have you worried?" Violet asked, taking Nate from him when the baby reached out for her.

"Nothing in particular, just being cautious."

"Can't fault you there," she said with another smile that made his heart almost stop. "But let's eat first. These do smell delicious." She pointed to the cinnamon rolls she'd placed on the counter. Keeping Nate perfectly balanced, she located plates and coffee mugs in the cabinets. "Everything we need."

It seemed as if that were true, but he didn't want to get too comfortable. That led to complacency, which would be dangerous for all of them. After breakfast, he'd complete a thorough risk analysis of the house, yard, and neighborhood. He could bet that Rogers's firm had already done so, but he'd never been one to rely on someone else's work.

If he found any gaps in the security, he'd make sure they were plugged right away.

7

Anderson settled onto the couch next to Violet and waited for the video image to come up on the laptop. They were going to talk to Rogers and begin the process of sorting out their situation. Nate reached out to grab Anderson's arm, leaving a trail of water on his skin. The boy sat on Violet's lap, drooling and chewing on a plastic ring.

"He's teething," Violet explained, using a washcloth to wipe the drips from Nate's chin.

"So that makes him a leaky faucet." Anderson was adjusting to being around a baby, but it was new territory. The day before, he had nervously watched over a napping Nate while Violet ran to a store to purchase groceries and baby supplies. She'd returned with countless bags of stuff that she'd stowed away in the safe house's closets and cabinets. Violet was organized, which he appreciated.

"According to the books and my mom, yes," she said. "We can expect this to continue for a while."

"Great," Anderson muttered, and she bumped her knee against his.

"It's what babies do." She gave him a pointed look.

"If you say so," he said as Rogers appeared on the screen. It had been five years since he'd seen Lt. Commander Dan Rogers, but he hadn't changed. His hair was a bit grayer, but his eyes were still the piercing blue Anderson remembered from his early days as a SEAL. He'd been assigned to Rogers's team, and the older man had put him through his paces. Even now, he felt the urge to stand and salute.

"Good to see you, Anderson," Rogers began.

"Thank you, sir. Good to see you as well. I appreciate your help."

"I never turn down a fellow SEAL in need." Rogers shifted his attention to Violet. "This must be Violet DiPaula."

"Commander Rogers. It's nice to meet you," Violet said, giving his former CO a smile. "Thank you for finding us a place to stay."

"Not a problem," Rogers replied. "I've read the report my associate put together, but suppose you tell me everything, from your time together in Russia to now."

Over the next thirty minutes, Anderson and Violet took turns explaining their mission, the security breach at Violet's agency, the threats against her, and the attack that made them go on the run. Rogers nodded and asked pertinent questions several times.

"That jibes with everything I could learn," Rogers said when they finished. "My concern is that the breach wasn't fully plugged, which may have been intentional."

"What?" Anderson said, shooting Violet a look. She seemed unsurprised by this bit of information. An intentional security leak? What kind of fool would allow that?

She shrugged. "It happens in intelligence work. Sometimes we leave an avenue open to see where it leads."

"As far as I can tell, that's what's happened," Rogers confirmed. "Which means neither of you can log into any systems you may have access to. Everything you do there might be traced and lead the bad guys directly to you."

"That's what I expected." Violet shifted Nate on her lap, deftly trading the ring for another toy.

"So you've got to sit tight for now and let us work. As soon as I have something to share, I'll get it to you in either encrypted files or some kind of drop. Whichever seems safest."

"I appreciate that, sir," Anderson said.

"I'll be in contact." Rogers signed off the call, and the room was silent for a moment.

"There's really nothing we can do?" Anderson asked. He hated sitting around and waiting for something to happen. He was much more the type to go make it happen, to force a situation along. And, frankly, he was bored. In the two days they'd been in the safe house, he'd learned every inch of the structure and yard, including anything he perceived as a weak spot in the home's defense. He'd adjusted camera angles on the security system and run diagnostics. He'd been hoping the meeting with Rogers would give him a direction to follow.

"Not nothing," Violet said, rising to her feet with the baby in her arms. "We need to make dinner, and I'll cut you a deal. I'll cook if you entertain this guy." She tapped Nate on the nose, making him giggle.

Anderson hesitated. Over the past two days, he'd learned that babies ran on a type of cycle. The sequence varied some, but it included five basic elements: eat, poop, play, cry, nap. Crying had been at a minimum since they'd arrived, thankfully, but the other four behaviors drove the day's schedule. Anderson had gotten more comfortable with caring for Nate, even managing to change a poopy diaper while Violet was in the shower. He'd viewed it as a task that had to be completed, which would have been great if Nate hadn't viewed his time on the changing pad as an opportunity to thrash his legs and squirm. Even with that, Anderson had accomplished the task without incident. It was a positive, a win.

"You can do this," Violet said. "I'll be one room away. If you like, we can set up a code word you can yell if you need help." He didn't remember her teasing him this way when they'd worked together in Moscow. That had been all business and tension. Having a kid with someone sure did change the dynamics.

"What are you thinking for dinner?" he asked.

"Chicken Florentine over wild rice. I might even whip up a dessert."

"Here." Anderson reached for his son. "I'll take him." His mouth was already watering at the thought of the meal. He could manage solo care of Nate with good food as a reward.

Violet kissed Nate's forehead and set him on Anderson's lap before heading to the kitchen.

"Just us, kid. You've got to promise to be good," Anderson said.

Nate gave him a gummy grin and babbled incoherently. At least he didn't cry when his mother walked away. That was a plus. Anderson transferred the baby to the blanket spread on the living room floor, using a special pillow to prop him up. Violet had a name for the doughnut-shaped pillow, but he couldn't remember what it was.

Anderson pulled the basket of toys closer and found a ball. He handed it to Nate, who rubbed the ball over his face before tossing it aside.

Anderson retrieved the ball and returned it to Nate, who repeated his action.

"Okay, not a ball day. Let's try something else." Anderson dug three cups that nested inside each other from the basket. "Check these out, buddy." He showed the baby how the cups could go together or separate and gave Nate two of them to play with. Nate banged them against each other, and Anderson winced at the noise. "Not their intended use."

When Anderson tried to take the cups from the boy's hands, Nate's lower lip stuck out, a look Anderson already recognized as the precursor to a crying fit. Anderson hastily released the cups. "God, I wish you could talk," he said. "That would make this easier." Nate clanked the cups together again and giggled.

"Yeah, that's funny for you, but I'm lost." He ran a hand through his hair. "Sh—oot, I speak seven languages, and I can't communicate with my own kid." Anderson eyed the boy. "Maybe there's another way." During some of his online research about babies over the past few days, Anderson had come upon an article about teaching sign language to kids. The article had been focused on toddlers, but it was worth a try. "Okay, stay with me."

Anderson signed "hello" several times by moving his hand to his head in a salute-like gesture. Nate watched, rocking back and forth against his pillow, but made no attempt to imitate the motion. "Let's try another one. How about "yes"?" Anderson closed his fist and tipped it forward and back, but to no avail. At least he was entertaining Nate, who was happily watching him. "I think you're enjoying my parental struggles. I thought only teenagers did that."

Anderson took a minute to reevaluate. "Maybe if I help you." He took the baby's hands in his and tried to move his fingers to create the words. "See, you have to bend all your fingers." Anderson was careful to keep his touch gentle as he manipulated the boy's hands.

"Okay, that's better." He released Nate's hands after getting his fingers in the correct position. "You try it." Anderson leaned closer, hoping his teaching had taken root, but Nate just wiggled his hands in Anderson's face and laughed. Anderson couldn't help his smile. "Okay, I admit defeat. You're too young."

"Too young for what?" Violet asked from the doorway that led to the kitchen.

Anderson felt his face turn hot. He hadn't expected an audience. "I was trying to teach him sign language. I thought it might bridge the communication gap, but it's not working." He pulled Nate into his lap and leaned back against the couch.

"He'll get it eventually. You should keep trying."

As she looked at him, the meaning of her words sank in for both of them. Anderson wasn't going to be around "eventually." If they weren't in this situation, Anderson would have nothing to do with either of them.

"Maybe you could teach me," she suggested, breaking the unspoken tension, "and I'll share the knowledge with him when he's older." She plopped down opposite Anderson. "We've got a little time before dinner's ready."

"Are you sure?" Anderson asked.

"Of course. I'm always glad to learn another language. It'll put me closer to catching up with you." She smiled. Her language skills were equal to his, but it had been a point of competition between them. "I'll just need one more after you teach me ASL."

He gave a nod and went through basic greetings, teaching her how to introduce herself and ask someone else's name. Nate grabbed play-fully at Anderson's moving hands before falling asleep against him.

A beeping from the kitchen interrupted them. "That's the oven timer." Violet rose gracefully from the floor. How'd she make that look so easy?

Anderson started to shift around. "I'll help—"

"Please don't," she said in a low voice, stopping his movement. "He didn't nap earlier, and he really needs this sleep. Let him stay with you, and I'll bring you a plate. Beer?"

"That would be great." He watched her leave the room, enjoying the slight sway of her hips and the way she flipped her hair back over her shoulders. Living with her, he was constantly reminded of the attraction that had brought them together in Moscow. She held an appeal for him that was different from his reaction to other women he'd been with, which he found confusing and irritating. He didn't want a relationship with her or anyone else, but something about her tugged at him.

In a few minutes, she returned holding two plates, and a bottle of beer in the crook of one arm. He took the beer from her, but he couldn't figure out how he'd manage a plate and fork, since Nate had one of his arms pinned.

"Maybe if you cut up my food, I can manage," he said after taking a drink of the beer and setting it aside.

"I can feed you." She sat facing him, close enough that their knees bumped.

"What?" His heart rate spiked. That would be way too intimate. "No, you don't need to do that. I can eat later."

"Don't trust me?" She gave him a taunting smile. "I promise I won't spill on you."

"I wasn't worried about that."

"Then what were you worried about?" Her expression was all innocence. "I'll be hurt if you don't try this recipe. It's a favorite of mine."

"It smells good," he admitted with a glance at the plate.

"Give it a try." She lifted a forkful of chicken and rice to his mouth. "Open up."

Like a child, he obeyed and let her feed him the delicious meal. She took her time, alternating forkfuls for him and for herself, allowing them both to savor the food. They didn't talk much, not wanting to disturb the sleeping baby. When both plates were empty and he'd finished his beer, she came closer, her face only inches from his.

"You've got a little sauce…" She flicked her finger along his lower lip, and their eyes met. Hers glowed with an inner light that he could only interpret as desire. She stroked his cheek with a softness that surprised him. "Anderson?" The word held a thousand meanings, but only an action could be the response.

He caught her hand in his and kissed her fingertips, never breaking eye contact with her. He heard a slight hitch in her breathing and smiled at her. "Kiss me," he said.

She raised an eyebrow, and he thought she might retreat, but she was too fearless for that. A second passed before she pressed her lips to his and her hands went around his neck. The kiss was slow and gentle, unlike the previous ones they'd shared. She sighed, just a whisper of sound, but it did things to him, and he wanted to wrap his arms around her and lower her to the floor.

But the baby… Nate stirred against him, making Anderson break the kiss. The boy stretched as he woke and focused on his mother. His chubby face crinkled into a smile.

"Hi, baby, did you have a good nap?" Violet's voice was still throaty from the kiss. She rested one hand on Anderson's shoulder and the other on the baby's head.

It was a personal moment, a family moment. Anderson felt something like panic rise in his chest. He wasn't cut out for this. "You take him," Anderson said, thrusting Nate at Violet, "and I'll do the dishes."

He caught her expression. He expected to see hurt at his abrupt departure, but all he saw was pity. Somehow, that was a thousand times worse.

8

———————

The following morning, Anderson followed the scent of freshly brewed coffee to the kitchen. Violet sat at the table with Nate in her lap. She had one arm around the baby and was bouncing her leg to keep him occupied while she scanned the laptop screen.

"There's fruit salad in the fridge," she said, looking up with a smile, "and yogurt."

"You've been up for a while," he commented as he poured a cup of coffee and topped off her mug. He'd cleaned the kitchen the evening before, after their kiss. He'd needed something to do, because it was best if he didn't think too much about that kiss. He'd never known that a kiss could be both passionate and gentle. It had been startling in an entirely good way, but the new territory made him uncomfortable. Overnight, he'd spent plenty of time staring at the ceiling of the small bedroom he'd set up for himself. In the light of day, he had to put their shared dinner and kiss out of his mind—or playing house with Violet would become even more difficult than it already was.

"This guy," she said, tweaking Nate's foot, "decided that four a.m. was morning."

"Sorry about that," Anderson muttered, feeling responsible for his son's actions. "You could have woken me."

She gave a one-shoulder shrug. "I'm used to it, and it gave me a chance to start working my way through this data." An encrypted hard drive had arrived by courier late the evening before. The drive was now connected to the laptop, and Violet kept switching between tabs as she studied the material.

"Figure anything out?" he asked.

"Not yet. It's going to take time. Rogers gathered a lot of intel on short notice."

"He's good at that. Do you want me to take Nate?" He'd committed to doing what he could to help her and get them both out of this situation as quickly as possible. Then he could figure out his relationship to her and Nate. The panic about his role as a father hadn't relented. Despite that, though, he felt an unexpected willingness to assist with Nate.

Violet dropped a kiss on the baby's head. "I've got him. Get some breakfast, and then I think he'll be ready for a morning nap."

Anderson put together a plate of fruit, granola, and yogurt and ate while Violet worked. He didn't interrupt her, knowing that she worked best in silence. He'd gotten accustomed to her habits during their assignment in Moscow. If he talked or even ate too loudly, she'd scowl at him. He'd seen that expression plenty during those weeks… but she'd softened some, it seemed.

Motherhood? Maybe, he decided, as she continued to keep Nate happy by tickling his stomach or making soft soothing sounds when he got restless.

She had this under control, and there was nothing he hated more than feeling useless. Neither she nor Nate seemed to need him, and it might be hours before she was ready to share her projections with him. He needed a task to occupy his time. He glanced out the kitchen window into the backyard. An overgrown hedge caught his attention. It could do with a pruning; small branches stuck out of it at odd angles. He recalled seeing some garden tools in the shed. A service hired by Rogers's firm mowed the lawn, but there was still work Anderson could do outside.

"I'm going to go work in the yard," he said, rising from his seat.

"Huh? Sure." Violet's eyes barely focused on him.

"Yell if you need me or figure out something interesting." With one last glance at her, he went through the door and made his way to the tool shed. Working in the yard would be perfect. He'd be too impatient if he stayed in the house, and it was good for their cover.

He'd noticed on his trips through the neighborhood that the lawns were carefully maintained. The men of the households seemed to hold dominion, spending time trimming and mowing after work. He looked through the tools, able to identify most of them. Even though he'd owned a house in Hartsville for the past year, he'd been gone on missions nearly the entire time, so he'd hired a service to maintain the lawn.

He'd always wanted to do it himself, though. That had been his plan when he purchased the house. Growing up, he'd had no one to show him how to do any of this—nor a yard to do it in—but he'd had an interest, which had been stoked by watching YouTube videos and HGTV. Here was his opportunity, he decided, as he grabbed pruners and walked to the hedge that divided the safe house's yard from the one next door.

The sun rose higher in the sky and the day got warmer while Anderson worked, but he didn't mind. Getting the hedge under control led to other tasks. After lunch, he cleared out what must have been a vegetable garden at one point, pulled weeds, and edged the front sidewalk.

Late in the afternoon, he was surveying the low-hanging branch of an oak tree when a man came from the neighboring house and walked toward him. Anderson's guard went up automatically, but it seemed unlikely an enemy had infiltrated the neighborhood enough to be in residence. While staying alert, he returned the guy's affable smile.

"Hi, I'm Jeff Yates," the man, still dressed in a suit and tie from work, said with an outstretched hand.

"Anderson Lee. Nice to meet you." He returned the handshake.

"Everyone around here's glad this house is finally occupied. You renting it?"

Anderson hadn't thought that part through, but it made sense for his and Violet's cover. "That's right."

"I thought as much, since it never went on the market." Jeff surveyed the front yard. "You've done a lot today."

"Yeah, I had some free time. Is this tree on your side of the property line or mine?" Anderson indicated the oak.

"Technically yours," Jeff said. "It could do with a trim."

"That's what I was thinking." The oak's branches scraped against both houses. The sound had woken Anderson during their first night there, and he'd prowled around the exterior until he located the problem.

"I'll give you a hand if you like," Jeff offered. "It won't take long with the two of us."

Anderson hesitated only a second. Accepting help wasn't easy for him, but this seemed like a good opportunity to learn more about the neighborhood, which might come in handy. "That'd be great."

"Let me change and grab my saw," Jeff said as he headed for his garage.

Working together, Anderson and Jeff trimmed the tree while Jeff chatted about the other people who lived on the block and the get-togethers they sometimes had. It was all foreign to Anderson, who'd never had that sense of community in the civilian world. His past had taught him to distrust others, especially when they seemed overly nice, but he didn't get any negative vibes from Jeff.

"Hello, Mr. Conklin," Jeff said to an elderly man with a wide-brimmed straw hat who came down the sidewalk, then he introduced Anderson.

"I saw you turning over the dirt in the vegetable patch," the newcomer said, "and thought you might need some seeds." Mr. Conklin thrust a handful of seed packets into Anderson's hand. "Remember to give them a light watering after you've planted. Bye."

Anderson was staring after the man when Jeff chuckled. "I wasn't used to people being so friendly when I moved here either. I grew up in a place where making eye contact was unwise, but it's different here in the burbs."

"So it seems," Anderson agreed.

"You get used to it," Jeff said, but Anderson knew he wouldn't be around long enough for that to happen. He and Violet would move on as soon as the threat was neutralized—or the safe house became compromised.

"Yeah. I guess I will. Thanks for your help." Anderson held up the seeds. "I better get these in the ground."

"See you later."

After Jeff left, Anderson returned to the backyard and began establishing rows for the different seeds. Lettuce, carrots, green beans. It didn't matter that he wouldn't be here to eat any of it. The act of planting a garden made him feel connected to someplace. Not a sensation he was used to, but he liked it.

As he finished planting a row of beans, he heard the back door slam. Violet was making her way toward him with Nate on her hip and a grim expression on her face. He tensed. Something was wrong.

"What is it?" he asked.

She blew out a sigh and put Nate down on the grass at her feet before answering. "Based on what I'm seeing, our predicament is worse than I thought. I have the satisfaction of being right about one thing, though."

"What's that?" He took a quick glance around to make sure no one could hear them.

"We're both being targeted. It was no coincidence that the attack came when we were together. The real problem is that the tear in the agency's security network is bigger than I would have imagined. The breach wasn't a little data. It was a ton of classified, compromising intel." She didn't have to add that both of them were totally exposed. That was obvious. "I notified Rogers's guys and asked them to track a few more leads for me. Other than that, I'm stuck." She rubbed a hand over her face in frustration.

"What about notifying your bosses?" he suggested, although he didn't like the idea much.

"That's what I wanted to talk with you about," she said. "I think it's too much of a risk to reach out to them."

"I agree." The more people who knew where they were, the greater the danger. For himself he wouldn't much care. If it were up to him, he'd taunt whoever this enemy was to bring the situation to a turning point—but he couldn't do that with Violet and Nate depending on him to protect them. Running security for Violet in Moscow had been a challenge, partly because of the chemistry between them. Adding Nate to the mix, though, altered everything. "So we've done all we can for now."

"You're right," she said, but the rigidness of her posture didn't change. She needed something to get her mind off their problem.

"Do you want to help me plant the rest of these seeds?" He still had two packets left, and he held them up. "We've got pumpkins and sweet corn."

"I've never grown either of those." A little light returned to her eyes. "My mom and I always kept an herb garden when I was a kid. I plan to do the same with Nate. It's important to understand where food comes from."

Anderson had never thought of it that way, but it made sense. It helped to create the connection he'd felt when cutting back the tree with Jeff. If he got to a store, he'd pick up some seeds for herbs and maybe clear a patch just off the back deck where they'd be handy to pick and cook with. He glanced toward the house and mentally selected a spot. He was about to tell Violet about his plan when reality hit.

They wouldn't be there to see any of these seeds be more than sprouts, because none of this was real. He didn't have a real relationship with Violet or Nate. This wasn't his house and garden. It was all fake, for the purpose of escaping a threat to their lives. Any good vibes, any sense of domesticity he'd been feeling washed out of him in an instant.

He looked down in time to see Nate pick up a fistful of dirt from the edge of the garden and smear it over his face.

"Stop!" Anderson yelled, making the baby look up and tears come to his eyes. "He ate dirt!"

Violet dropped to her knees alongside the child and took him onto her lap. "Uh-oh," she said in a singsong voice, apparently unbothered. "No eating dirt, little man."

"Should we call…" Anderson had no idea who to call. A doctor, the hospital, poison control?

"He's fine," she said and then chuckled.

What the hell was funny? Anderson knelt next to them and saw his son's expression. Nate had opened his mouth wide, and his face was scrunched in displeasure.

"That doesn't taste good, does it?" Violet swiped his mouth out with her finger and used the edge of her T-shirt to get some of the dirt off his face.

"Will he be okay?" Anderson's heart rate was slowly coming down, but he still felt the need to take action.

"It's just dirt," she said before addressing the child. "My grandma always said, 'God made dirt, and dirt don't hurt'… except that it tastes icky."

Nate gave her a smile, clearly over his upset, and basked in the attention Violet lavished on him. Anderson had never had that. Never had a mother who comforted him and knew what to do. His mother had viewed him as someone who could get her a beer from the fridge so she didn't have to get up. Other than that, he was a hell of an inconvenience. She'd never bandaged a bloody knee or attended a school event.

How much easier it must be for a kid whose parent knew how to wash away real and metaphorical dirt. Anderson's dirt had always been his own to deal with, which had forced him to toughen up young. He'd survived and done well for himself, but it wasn't something he'd wish on others.

Nate was lucky to have Violet. Anderson felt warmth and calm grow inside him at her motherliness. Nate would always have someone he could depend on.

"I better give him a bath," she said, rising with Nate in her arms.

"I'll finish up here and be in to help you." Anderson saw surprise cross her face. She hadn't expected his offer of assistance.

"Okay," she said, giving him a smile.

Anderson couldn't stop himself from watching her walk to the house. She was an impressive woman in so many ways.

9

———————

Violet kicked off her sandals as she entered the house, making straight for the bathroom while considering her options. She hadn't bought a baby bathtub, and none of the sinks in the house were big enough to give Nate a bath in. The day before she'd gotten in the regular tub with him.

She balanced Nate on one hip as she started lukewarm water flowing into the tub, then removed Nate's soiled clothes and diaper. He was extra squirmy, and she didn't want to put him down on the bathroom floor.

"Well, I think I'll get in with you, clothes and all." She evaluated her running shorts and T-shirt. A little water wouldn't hurt them any. Grabbing the baby wash, she got into the tub and propped Nate between her knees. "Ready to get clean, baby boy?"

She gently washed his hair and face, removing the last traces of the dirt. She'd scrub the rest of him in a minute, after she let him play. Nate splashed his hands in the water and squealed with delight.

"Your daddy likes the water, too, or I think he does." She'd known Anderson in landlocked Moscow, but he was a SEAL, and by definition they spent time in the water during training and missions. "We'll have to ask him about that."

Living in the safe house with Anderson was a surprising bonus for her, because it gave her an opportunity to see him differently. Even if he wouldn't be present in her and Nate's life, she'd have some stories to tell Nate when he asked about his daddy later.

"Come in," she called when a knock sounded on the bathroom door. Anderson pushed the door open, and his eyes widened in surprise. "What?" she asked with a grin. "Never seen anyone take a bath with all her clothes on?"

"Not what I was expecting," he said, making her wonder what he had expected.

As a matter of fact, why had he offered to help anyway? For a man who claimed he wasn't interested in fatherhood, he sure seemed to be making an effort. She formed a quick plan to take advantage of that.

"I can't promise you won't get wet," she said, "but if you want to learn how to give him a bath, this is a good time."

"Sure." Anderson stripped off his shirt and knelt by the tub.

Violet reminded herself to keep her attention on the task at hand. A shirtless Anderson was enough to distract most any woman. "I've already washed his hair and face, but he's still plenty dirty." She tickled Nate under the chin. "Aren't you, babe?"

"Tell me what to do," Anderson said, rubbing his hand over the baby's clean hair.

"Add a little soap to the washcloth," she said, handing him the wet cloth, "and start cleaning. I usually start from the top and go down to the toes. Be careful not to scrub too hard. Baby skin is delicate." Anderson cautiously started wiping down Nate's neck and torso. "That's it. You've got it. He's way easier to wash now that he's bigger. Newborns are tough to bathe."

"And you were on your own." Anderson was so focused on washing Nate's back that she couldn't tell whether he felt any regret over having missed that time with Nate or if his words were just an observation.

"My mom came for his birth," she said, "and she stayed with me for the first two weeks. I don't know what I would have done without her."

"I'm glad you weren't alone," he said, beginning on Nate's legs.

"Now, I'm never alone," she quipped. Having a baby made even simple things more challenging, but she couldn't imagine being without him now. He was truly a bundle of joy.

"Is that a problem?" Anderson looked up at her.

"Not at all." She smiled at his question. "I love him."

Anderson nodded and went back to bathing Nate before saying, "He's lucky to have you."

"I'm lucky to have him," she said softly, wondering who this Anderson was. He wasn't quite the man she'd known in Moscow. She watched him as he scrubbed between Nate's toes. Anderson was the same in some ways. Intense and dedicated to the job, protective. In other ways, though, he was all new to her.

"I think he's clean." Anderson rocked back on his heels and reached for a towel she'd put nearby.

"Usually he likes to play in the tub, but he seems a bit sleepy. I'll bet he'd take a nap long enough for us to eat dinner without him. Would you get him dressed and put him in the crib while I…" She gestured to her soaked clothes.

"Sure, and take your time. I've got him." Anderson wrapped the baby in the towel after Violet lifted him from the tub.

Violet listened until she heard Anderson talking to Nate in the baby's room before hopping out of the tub herself. If he was willing to watch their son for a while, she was going to take a genuine bath. She stripped off her wet clothes and added hot water and a lavender-scented bath bomb to the tub before getting back in.

Heavenly, she thought as she sank in up to her neck. She'd only taken a few baths since Nate's birth, and always with the baby monitor by her side. No need for that today. Time in the tub did a lot to erase her worries about the threat against them—at least temporarily. She felt the tension in her shoulders ease as she reminded herself that she and Anderson worked well as a team. Together, they could manage anything, despite their differences.

Could they manage parenting? That was a complex question. She lacked the data to make an accurate projection, so she might as well not worry about it. Putting any serious thoughts out of her head for a while, she relaxed deeper into the tub until the water started to cool. Then she dried off and put on the terry cloth robe she'd left on a hook, before making her way to her room for a change of clothes. She'd just pulled shorts and a shirt out of a drawer when she saw Anderson in the doorway. She watched his gaze travel from her legs up to her face.

"Is Nate okay?" she asked, perusing his bare chest where every muscle was defined. Her fingers tingled, remembering what it had felt like to run her hands over his hard body.

"He went out like a light after I rocked him for a few minutes," he said, walking into the room.

"Good," she said and waited. Was there something else on Anderson's mind? She thought so. Last night during their kiss, she'd sensed he'd wanted more. She'd definitely wanted him, even if it wasn't smart to go down that road. For most of the day, she'd kept focused on her work and tucked away how that kiss had reawakened the passion she'd felt for him. She could no longer do that when he was standing in her bedroom.

The question was this: Who would make the first move?

"We could make dinner," he suggested, "or we could pick up where we left off last night."

She felt a little breathless just thinking about what could happen between them. "Will we be able to stop at kissing?"

"Not if it's up to me, which means I should probably walk out of here right now." He came to stand in front of her instead of heading for the door. "Except I don't want to do that."

She tossed the clothes she was holding on top of the dresser and reached for him, running one finger down his chest. When they'd had sex in Moscow, it had been intense, dynamic, and oh, so good. Everything about this moment felt different. The same desire was there, but the room was charged with a different array of emotions. Ones she couldn't so easily name but had to act on.

She loosened the tie of her robe and, with a shrug, let it drop to the floor. His gaze traveled over her again, and she wondered what he was thinking. "Remember, I've had a baby," she said. Her body had changed in ways that he was sure to notice.

"You're more beautiful than ever." His voice was a whisper as his eyes came back to hers. "Should we try a bed this time?"

"I think that would be… nice," she said and took his hand to lead him to her bed. She pulled back the covers, got in, and watched while he removed his shorts, baring the rest of his beautiful body.

"Condoms?" he asked before joining her.

She laughed and tilted her head in the direction of Nate's room. "That didn't work for us, but it's okay. I'm on the pill now, and I'm STI negative." She'd had routine tests during her pregnancy, and she hadn't had sex since the night Nate was conceived.

"Me, too. Well, not the pill part," he said with a chuckle. He sat on the edge of the bed and touched her hair, fanned out across the pillow.

She wanted to ask if he'd been with anyone since her, but she didn't have the right. She wasn't his wife or girlfriend. She was his baby mama. Not a bad title, but it came without privileges.

"I don't remember this," he said, lightly touching the tattoo on her left side. "A bluebird. Very pretty."

"It was dark," she said, referring to their sexual encounter in Moscow, "and we were in a hurry."

"No hurry this time."

If he wanted to take it slow, that was fine with her, but she wanted him closer. She patted the bed next to him.

He took the hint and lay on the bed but then surprised her by wrapping an arm around her waist and pulling her on top of him. She could feel every inch of him, including the erection that pushed into her stomach. This was perfect. She loved the feel of his warm skin under hers.

"Where were we last night?" He stroked his fingers over her cheek and along her lower lip.

"Kissing, but we had more clothing on," she teased as she combed the hair back from his temple.

"Not by choice." He chuckled, and then his face became serious as he studied her. She thought he might not speak again. "Kiss me," he finally said, echoing his demand from the previous night.

She lowered her lips to his and let the kiss speak for her. They kissed for a long time, almost as if they were becoming reacquainted. At first, it was light, but as the kiss deepened, his hands stroked down her back, kneading her skin and increasing her desire. She rubbed against him, and he broke the kiss with a moan.

She lowered her head and kissed down his neck to his chest, running her tongue over his flat nipples and enjoying the hitch in his breathing. Slowly, she moved farther down him, kissing and licking. When she'd nearly reached his erection, he rolled her onto her back.

"Hey! I was just getting to the good part," she said, and immediately sucked in a breath when his mouth closed over her nipple. It felt as good as she remembered from that hectic, passion-driven episode. This slow seduction was better, though. This was making love, not having sex. Did he feel that way, too?

"This *is* good." His words were muffled against her skin as he moved his lips over her. "I've been dreaming of this."

She'd had dreams about him as well, so many she'd lost count. The reality of him as a lover was far better. She closed her eyes and concentrated on what he was doing as he continued to move down her body. She felt a kiss on her hip bone, another just below her navel, one on the inside of her thigh. A rush of moist heat flooded between her legs, and then she felt his tongue part her, felt it swirl over her cunt. He'd done that to her in Moscow, but then it had been a form of erotic torture. Now, he was trying to please her with his gentle, evocative strokes.

"I want you inside me," she murmured, on the verge of coming.

He stilled before placing a last kiss on her cunt, then took his time as he came back to her, his mouth coasting up her body until they were face-to-face. She arched up, initiating another kiss as she wrapped her legs around him, silently asking for what they both wanted. Without breaking the kiss, he entered her, and she gasped at the fullness.

They moved together, skin rubbing on skin, as the rhythm built and she felt an intense coiling inside her that was waiting to release. One more thrust, one more stroke and she came. She held him tighter to her, letting the orgasm play out. He pushed into her again, and she felt him throb and pulse before he buried his head in her hair and whispered her name, over and over.

A minute later, he rolled off her but pulled her with him so they lay together on their sides facing each other. It was intimate and beautiful. Violet snuggled into him and rested her head on the pillow by his. She valued her independence, but this connection between them was too strong to ignore. She didn't even try to resist the force that seemed to bring them together.

If only it would last beyond their time at the safe house.

No. She couldn't let herself go there. Now was enough.

10

———————

few days later, Violet took advantage of some quiet time to straighten up. She moved through the kitchen putting dishes away before heading to the dining room, which they only used as a space to work. The laptop, hard drive, and a legal pad where she'd written some notes were on the shiny surface.

When she picked up her legal pad, she spied one of Anderson's small notebooks beneath it. Unusual for it to be out of his pocket, she thought, as she picked it up and turned it over in her hands. She was curious—what did he record? She listened but didn't hear him in the house. He must still be in the backyard with Nate. She'd just take a peek.

She flipped open the notebook at the halfway point, focusing on a page of handwritten text. His notes appeared to be in sort of code. She studied it for a minute, looking for patterns and clues how to interpret it. It seemed to be a blend of several languages. She saw Russian, Arabic, and Spanish, but it was more complicated than that. She looked closer. After a few minutes she caught on to some of it. He

77

rendered English words using foreign alphabets. Clever. It would take time and a vast knowledge of language to understand it all.

She continued toward the back of the notebook and stopped at a random page where everything was in English. Starting to read, she smiled as she recognized the dirt-eating story and the subsequent bath. Anderson had recounted what happened, along with his fears and worries.

"How sweet," she murmured when she read Anderson's version of rocking his son to sleep while she was in the tub. The story ended there and didn't include the time they'd spent in her bed. That hour had been the best part of her day.

She felt a happy glow just remembering it. Since then, he'd joined her in the master bedroom each night. They hadn't discussed the future, because there were no answers—not easy ones, anyway. One day at a time, she reminded herself. Looking at it that way enabled her to enjoy being with him.

She continued on to the last entry in the notebook, about their picnic in the backyard from the day before. His account was surprisingly detailed. He seemed to paint a picture with his descriptions, as if he wanted something tangible to remember the experience by. Was this his way of expressing what he couldn't say?

When she heard footsteps in the kitchen, she quickly tucked the notebook away and busied herself sorting through some junk mail that had arrived at the house. A few seconds later, Anderson was in the doorway with Nate.

"Everything okay?" she asked, looking up.

"Yeah, but I thought I'd take Nate for a trip around the neighborhood. He's getting bored."

Anderson had gone from not knowing anything about babies to being able to perceive Nate's mood before he started fussing. Interesting, but she kept the observation to herself. If she said something, Anderson would be sure to deny it.

"Sure, that's a good idea," she said. A neighbor had loaned them a stroller when she saw they didn't have one.

"Lock up after me," Anderson said.

"I will." They were careful about locking doors and setting the alarm system. She noticed, though, that the neighbors didn't seem to worry about home security much. They came and went freely, without the constant vigilance she and Anderson had to maintain.

After she helped strap Nate into the stroller, she gave each of her boys a kiss and held the door for them. She sighed once they were on the sidewalk. She'd like to keep everything just like this... minus the threat against them. That she could do without.

She locked the door carefully, then noticed a message from her mom on her phone. She had some alone time, so she started a video call.

"Hi, Mom," she said as she went up the stairs to the bedroom. They'd been in touch enough that her mom knew she was safe but on the move.

"Hi, honey." Her mom smiled at her. "Is your situation any better?"

"Still in the middle of it, but no developments. We're safe." Seeing her mom helped give Violet a sense of normalcy. No matter what had happened in Violet's life, her mother had been there for her.

Her mother scrutinized her. "I'll take your word for that. How's my grandson?"

"He's doing fine. Thank goodness he's young, so he can't ask questions about why we're in a strange house." Disrupting a baby's schedule was no picnic, but she couldn't imagine trying to get an older child to understand the situation. Plus, Nate was too young to be scared as long as she and Anderson were calm around him.

"Can I see him, or is he napping?" her mom asked.

"Neither," Violet answered, sitting on the bed and propping herself against the headboard. "Anderson took him for a walk, but I'll send you a new picture later."

"Anderson is… doing okay with this?"

Violet had told her mother about the brief affair in Moscow and what she knew of Anderson, including her analysis that he wouldn't welcome being a father.

"Surprisingly well. He's jumped in with both feet and seems interested in caring for Nate. Not what I anticipated." What she didn't know was how long it would last.

"That's good, right?" her mother prompted.

"It is. I'm happy to be wrong about him, but…"

"But what, honey?" Her mother's expression was worried.

"He told me he didn't want to be a father," Violet said, remembering Anderson's immediate rejection of the idea. "He made that very plain the first day, so I'm afraid to trust his behavior now."

Her mom was quiet for a few seconds before speaking again. "You know words aren't always the best way for people to convey what's inside them."

"I do." Her work had taught Violet that. People's words weren't always the truth, because words sprang from fear, passion, or a hundred other emotions. Actions were the better indicator of what was inside someone, what their true feelings were. Anderson's actions had all indicated his ability to be a father.

But would he let himself be? That was a question she couldn't answer.

"And what about his actions toward you?" Her mother's tone was gentle.

The time in her bed suggested he was still attracted to her, but she didn't know what that meant beyond physical pleasure. Could he give her more than that? She didn't let herself imagine what shape that might take, because the temptation to believe they could be a normal, happy family was too great.

"He's been good to me, too," she admitted after a pause long enough for her mom to raise a questioning eyebrow. "Very good."

After they talked a bit more, she disconnected. Her mom's presence, even digitally, was always soothing. She was a practical, loving woman who had done her best by Violet. Violet knew she could follow her mom's example and raise Nate on her own, but she wondered if that was her only option. Anderson might…

She stopped her thoughts there, since she couldn't predict what he would do. Nevertheless, she felt good about the possibilities.

By eight that evening, any sense of harmony Violet possessed was shattered. Nate had been fine after his nap, but later in the afternoon, he turned fussy. At times, his cries became shrieks. He blew through diapers and outfits. She and Anderson took turns pacing the floor with him, skipping dinner altogether, while one of them took the baby and the other ran laundry and cleaned up the mess.

Violet called her pediatrician, who assured her that all babies have bad days, and it was probably teething or something mild, since Nate didn't have a fever. The pediatrician promised to check in again in the morning. That was only marginally comforting, considering Nate's obvious distress.

Finally too exhausted to cry any more, Nate rested his head against Violet's shoulder and dropped into a sound sleep. From there, she managed to put him in his crib without waking him. She and Anderson waited, watching, until they were sure he was out, and then they retreated to the master bedroom. After flipping on the baby monitor, Violet sprawled on the bed in exhaustion, but Anderson paced the room.

"That was awful," he said.

"But he's okay, and it's over." She didn't add that there would be other nights like this. That was the nature of parenting at times.

"I'm not cut out for it." Anderson's voice was low but emphatic.

"Cut out for what?" she asked, but she already knew the answer.

Anderson gave her a bewildered look. "Taking care of a kid, being a dad."

"You did fine," she argued, sitting up. Her senses told her that this conversation was critical for him—for all of them.

"You don't know." He stopped pacing and faced her. "You don't know how close I came to walking out the door tonight." His face was pained, anger vibrating off him. She controlled her reaction to his mood, knowing that his anger was self-directed. It had nothing to do with her or Nate.

"I think that's a natural response to a crisis," she said carefully. "Fight or flight. Since there was no one to fight, wanting to get away was normal." She'd had those moments, too. Not this time, but a few months ago when Nate had been colicky and she'd been so tired.

"I'm trained to think differently," Anderson said. "I know when to fight and when to retreat, and I've never gotten that wrong. I had no idea what to do in this situation. If you hadn't been here, I…" His lips pressed into a straight line as if trying to hold in his emotions. "Look,

I come from a long line of shitty fathers. Tonight proved to me that I'm no better than they were."

She had to be very cautious about what she said next, so she took a minute. He seemed so lost, not at all what she was used to with him. He faced danger and difficulty with courage. She'd seen him do it. Fatherhood shouldn't have the power to trip him up.

She held out her hand to him and waited as he exhaled a long breath before coming to her. When he sat next to her, she twisted her body to face him.

"I spent a lot of time analyzing what kind of dad you'd be, and I sold you short. I've watched you these past days with Nate. You're good. You care for Nate, make him happy, and accept your part of the responsibility. Those are all fatherly qualities."

He shook his head and averted his eyes. She needed to do more to convince him, because he was so capable of being a dad. She'd seen the evidence with her own eyes.

"Okay, take a look at it from a different angle. You're cognizant of your failings, willing to admit that you were overwhelmed. Only people who are invested and dedicated to improving do that, because they know they aren't perfect. But they want to be." She hoped her argument made sense to him.

"You have your mom to show you what a mother should be, but—"

"You had no one," she interrupted. He swung his gaze back to her. "You think I didn't research you before we worked together in Moscow? Oh, I know about your family. Their dysfunction and how you pulled yourself out of that. You defied what some might have thought was your destiny. Our families, our genes don't determine what we do or who we are. We do." She tapped his chest. "You know that better than most. So it's up to you whether you'll be a good father or not."

He focused on where their hands were still joined, and she let the silence play out, even though she desperately wanted to say more. This was up to him.

"I don't know if I can be," he said after several minutes.

She wanted to reiterate her confidence in him. She didn't think he'd be able to hear it right then, so, she changed tactics. "Okay, can you keep helping me, at least? Doing what you've been doing?" That would be a start toward him taking a role in Nate's life and, maybe, hers.

He nodded. "I'm trying to make things easier for you."

"You've done that." She smiled at him. "We already knew we made a good team."

"We were successful," he said, giving her a grin, "but it wasn't always easy."

She laughed, thinking of their conflicts in Russia. "Partly because we're both bossy, *and* we wanted to rip each other's clothes off."

"That did create some tension."

"It created Nate, too," she said softly. Her darling boy wouldn't be with them if the attraction between her and Anderson hadn't been so great.

He didn't respond in words but pulled her down on the bed and covered her body with his, starting a slow kiss. She relaxed as he kissed her lips and framed her face with his hands. His thumbs stroked over her cheeks.

"I should be too tired…" she whispered against his lips.

"Are you?" he asked, lifting his head.

"Not at all." She lightly ran her fingers up his back. They didn't bother to talk after that as they slowly shed their clothing and moved together. Loving and kissing were all-important right then, which made this different from their other encounters. There was no hurry, no need to prove anything, nothing but a building desire that brought them together in mind, heart, and body.

When he finally entered her, only pleasing each other mattered. They came together in an orgasm so joyful it brought tears to her eyes. While their bodies were still calming, he kissed her cheeks where the tears had run and she smiled at him, not having to explain that the tears didn't come from sadness. He seemed to understand, and she'd never felt closer to anyone.

Afterward, they spooned together with his arms wrapped around her. With his body tight to hers, she dropped into a deep, contented sleep.

11

Anderson rolled over and reached for his phone on the nightstand. The buzz of an incoming text had brought him out of a dreamless sleep. His need to rest wasn't a surprise after last evening. Nate's illness had been frustrating and exhausting, and the conversation with Violet afterward was one of the most blunt and emotional ones of his life. He didn't know what to think of it. Making love to her, though, had been the highlight of the night, possibly the year. He didn't want to admit there was something between them, but it was becoming increasingly difficult to pretend otherwise. She made him feel… whole, somehow. No one had ever had that effect on him. He hadn't allowed them to, and he shouldn't now. But Violet…

He gave himself a shake and glanced at the text from Allen Zimmerman, one of Rogers's men.

New developments. Use Wiffy.

Anderson got out of bed, for the first time realizing that he was alone. He listened for a second and heard Violet singing softly in Nate's room. All seemed peaceful, so he went to the living room where he'd left Wiffy, the encrypted phone Rogers's security company had placed in the house for them. A request to communicate via Wiffy was probably not a good sign.

He hit the only number programmed in the phone and waited for it to ping off multiple cell towers, making it more difficult to trace or listen in to conversations. After a minute, Allen answered.

"Thanks for checking in." Allen got down to business quickly. "Our night-shift monitoring guys picked up some intel that set off alarms. We're going to need you to move, but we don't have a house available yet."

Allen went on to explain how Russian mob communication in the area, though usually low, had suddenly increased. Rogers's team was looking into it. By itself that might not mean much, but the team had also followed some of the leads Violet uncovered regarding the data breach and had new concerns for their safety.

"So what's next?" Anderson asked. While listening to Allen, he'd prowled around the house, checking the defenses.

"We need to get you packets of intel for Violet to analyze—and new IDs. I can't risk dropping the material off directly to your location, because one of our techs found a worm in our system. He killed it fast, but it might be an indication that someone knows we're working with you. I don't want to lead the bad guys to your doorstep. You're going to have to go on a little scavenger hunt and retrieve the items yourselves."

"Is that safer?" They would be out and exposed. Anderson wasn't sure he liked that.

Anderson heard the man sigh. "We think it's the safest way, but you'll have to watch your back."

"Seems a little cloak-and-dagger," Anderson commented. "Is Rogers okay with this?" The method didn't seem in keeping with the former SEAL's usual caution.

"His order," Allen said. "Look, I know it's… unusual, but it's been a lifesaver in the past."

"All right," Anderson agreed, since he probably didn't have a choice. "Where am I headed?"

"Wiffy contains a secure app. We'll feed GPS coordinates and instructions to it one at a time. Once you retrieve one item, we'll make the next available."

"Got it," Anderson said.

"Good luck—and be careful," Allen said before hanging up.

Anderson found the app on the phone and went to check on Nate who —thankfully—seemed fine, then told Violet the plan. She too questioned the unusual method, but it had started to have some appeal for Anderson. They'd get out of the house and be taking action, which was better than biding their time being sitting ducks.

Half an hour later, they put Nate in the car and made their way to the first set of coordinates. Anderson took the elevator to the third floor of an office building in downtown Nashville. An office at the end of the hall had a mailbox attached to the door. What looked like an interoffice envelope was sticking from the box. Anderson retrieved it and retraced his steps to where Nate and Violet waited in the car. He hadn't liked leaving them, even for a few minutes, but a single man entering the building would gather less attention than a couple with a baby.

He handed the envelope to Violet as he climbed in. She undid the tie and pulled out a sheaf of papers while he checked the app and found a new message with the next coordinates.

"I'll read. You drive," she said and began flipping through pages.

"You're enjoying this," he commented as he wound his way out of downtown and made for the suburbs on the west side of the city.

"You know I love assessing new information," she said, not looking up.

"Anything good?" Anderson asked.

"It's definitely Volkhov's organization," she said, "but the question is who's calling the shots."

"Could be the Wolf himself, from prison." That wasn't unheard of in Russia, where the network of prisons was connected to the heart of the mob community.

"True, but someone must be directing the activity here." She flipped over a page and continued reading. "I like working with Rogers's team. They know how to get the goods. I've got descriptions and all known info for Volkhov's associates."

"Anybody ring a bell?" During their time in Moscow, they'd crossed paths with plenty of possible mobsters.

"I'm looking." She continued to sort through papers until they reached their next destination. There she'd have to participate, since the packet had been left in a fabric store.

"I have no idea how to locate this," he said, showing her the information on the encrypted phone. "McCall's M7718. Whatever the hell that means."

She didn't hesitate. "McCall's is the company name, and M7718 is the pattern number. Patterns are all stored in drawers, organized in numeric order."

He gave her a confused look. "You sew?"

"Me? No way, but I did help a friend pick out a pattern for a dress once." She put her hand on the door handle. "I'll be back in five."

She slipped from the car, and Anderson took a minute to scan their surroundings in the strip mall parking lot. Nothing seemed out of place, so he leaned over the seat to take a look at Nate. He was playing with his toes and looking around.

"Why couldn't you have been so calm last night, kid?" Anderson asked. Nate gave him a sloppy grin in response. "Never a dull moment with you, huh?"

Violet returned to the car a few minutes later and pulled a white packet from a bag. The outside was printed with the image of a model wearing a fancy dress. Again, she emptied the packet into her lap and began reading as he checked the phone and started driving.

"Our next stop is south of the city, at a house they're thinking of moving us to," he said. "They've stashed new IDs for us in a planter in front."

"Why aren't we moving there now?" she asked without looking up.

"I guess it's occupied." The message had said they were working on it. Rogers's team had steered them right so far, so he had to trust their judgment again.

Anderson kept his eyes on the road as they left the city and headed to a smaller town. He turned down a main street that looked like something out of an old movie, with its ornate façades and decorative light posts. Not a bad place to live. He turned off Main onto Pleasant Street and drove, keeping a lookout for number 343. He came to a stop sign and checked to his right. A black SUV sat at the curb.

He tensed. Anyone could own one of those, of course, but he didn't like coincidences. He turned left, his action catching Violet's attention.

"I thought the house was straight ahead," she said.

"It was. We might have company." He kept his eye on the SUV, but it didn't move. Probably nothing, but it was a good reminder that he needed to keep his guard up. Gathering clues in this way felt like a game, but it wasn't one. He took a loop around the block and came at number 343 from the opposite direction. He pulled to a stop three houses down and waited. No sign of the SUV or any other issues. He didn't like the location, though. The old neighborhood was beautiful but full of mature trees and tall hedges that blocked visibility.

"Stay here," he said to Violet. "I'm going to grab the IDs and be right back." He got out and headed up the street. Number 343 was a blue bungalow that sat back from the road under the canopy of a huge maple tree. As he reached its front walk, he felt his phone vibrate in his pocket. He thought of ignoring it, but something made him reach for it.

"The SUV just came around the corner," Violet said as soon as he answered. "Look right."

He swung his gaze in that direction and saw the black vehicle approaching at high speed. It slid to a stop thirty feet from him. Anderson felt torn. His training and instinct made him want to confront the bad guy, but he knew it was important to complete the mission: get the IDs they'd come for.

The SUV's door flew open, and a man in black tactical dress jumped out. Down the street, Violet was honking the horn, trying to create a distraction, but his opponent never took his eyes off Anderson.

A showdown. Bring it on, Anderson thought. And then he remembered the two people he'd pledged to protect. He hated backing down, but confronting this guy might put them at risk.

With a dip of his chin at the enemy, Anderson turned and sprinted to the car. By now, Violet was in the driver's seat and already had the vehicle rolling. He leaped in and they took off.

"Evasive driving," he said. "Take that corner." He pointed ahead. "We need to get out of this little town."

Violet wasted no time getting back to a highway. All the while, Anderson watched out behind them. He caught a glimpse of the black SUV once, but they lost it easily.

A little too easily, he worried. Did that mean the enemy didn't need to chase them because he knew where they were going?

It was a thought that made Anderson pledge to double down on security.

12

———————

Anderson waved to Jeff next door as they approached the driveway of the safe house. He'd had Violet circle their current street in loops, checking for the black SUV, before he determined it was safe to return.

"Out for a drive?" Jeff called when they got out of the car. "Beautiful day for it."

Anderson had been so focused on their mission that he'd hardly noticed the sun had come out after a cloudy morning.

"The baby had a doctor's appointment," Violet said, "and then we enjoyed some time at the park." She gave Jeff an easy smile. No one who heard or saw her would believe her words were false. She was a good operative.

"Is he okay?" Jeff's face held legitimate concern.

"Oh, yes," Violet responded. "He had a fussy night, and I was a little worried. New parents, you know how it is."

"I'm glad he's all right," Jeff said. "Take care."

Violet held Nate's hand up as if he was waving at Jeff before going into the house ahead of Anderson.

"Spare me nosy neighbors," Anderson commented after closing the door. "Nice cover, though."

"Seemed appropriate." She dropped her shoulder bag, where she'd stuffed the intel, on the dining room table.

As she reached into it, the doorbell rang. She froze, shooting Anderson a questioning look. He stepped to the front window and edged the drape back to see who was there.

"It's Kelly," he announced in an overly pleasant voice. "Hi, Kelly." Anderson opened the door and smiled at one of the women who had brought cinnamon rolls on their first morning in the neighborhood.

"Hi, I don't mean to be nosy, but did I hear you say the baby was sick?" Kelly poked her head in the door and spotted Violet.

Violet came from the dining room with Nate on her hip. "Not sick. Just a checkup. It's so kind of you to inquire."

Anderson was glad that Violet had it together. He was ready to yell at their neighbors to get off his lawn, then never open his door to anyone again. Couldn't people mind their own damn business?

"So glad to hear it," Kelly said. "And I wanted to let you know that we're having a potluck in the park on Saturday at five. We do it once a month during the summer. I hope you can come."

"We'd love to," Violet said, her expression showing enthusiasm for the idea. "Anything in particular we should bring?"

"A side dish or a dessert," Kelly said as she reached out to tickle Nate's bare feet. "The neighborhood association supplies burgers and hot dogs."

It was more information than Anderson needed or wanted. He could see good things about living in the suburbs—for most people, at least. It was a caring, family-oriented atmosphere. But, Christ, people were watching you all the time and forming judgments.

Anderson almost missed the rough-and-tumble trailer park of his youth. There, he'd known where he stood and when to expect trouble, which was often. People might have watched what you were doing, but they didn't feel the need to comment and interfere.

Until things reached a boiling point. He grimaced, remembering days when even riding the school bus had its dangers. He'd destroyed more than one metal lunch box using it as a weapon. Living in that environment had kept him on his guard. Living in a place like this had made him lower his defenses. He'd gone soft, and he was pissed about it.

And that had cost him earlier. The beautiful neighborhood where the IDs were hidden was idyllic, but danger had lurked there as it could anyplace. Trusting appearances was always a mistake. They'd almost gotten caught, and that was his fault. He couldn't let anything dull his senses again.

"Thanks. We'll be there," Violet said to Kelly as she closed the door on their company.

Anderson waited until he saw the woman cross the street to her house. "I hate living in a fishbowl. They probably know what we eat for dinner."

"She was being nice. And maybe a little nosy, but there was no harm in it." Violet handed Nate to him when the child reached out his arms.

"That may be true, but we're on a mission." He settled Nate against him, something that had become second nature. "We need to act like it." If they'd been anywhere else in the world, he'd have drawn his gun before answering the door.

"Have I been a security threat in some way?" she challenged. "Or broken protocol?"

"No," he had to admit. She'd been cautious, but he was rattled by their situation.

"We'll get through this," she said, relaxing. "Can you keep an eye on Nate until nap time? I want to look at this data more closely."

"I've got him." Anderson walked into the living room with Nate and used Wiffy to contact Allen Zimmerman again. He kept his voice low, so he didn't disturb Violet where she sat at the dining room table.

"How'd it go?" Allen asked without bothering with a greeting. "You made it to all three locations." Through the app on Wiffy, Rogers's team had been able to track their movements.

"We were unable to retrieve at the last one. We had company." He gave Allen a description of the vehicle and the man who'd been driving it. He'd wished he'd gotten closer, but he thought the man had a scar on his left cheek. That might help identify him.

"So you still need IDs," Allen said, cutting to the point. "I'll get some guys working on that and a new safe house for you. That one's compromised."

"No kidding," Anderson said, then moderated his tone. "I'm sorry. Thanks. I appreciate all your team is doing for us."

"Not a problem. Stay safe," Allen said and hung up.

"Stay safe, huh?" Anderson said to Nate, who was snuggled on his lap with his thumb in his mouth. "Like I was planning to put you in jeopardy."

Stay safe as a command always irritated Anderson. There were times in his life when he'd been reckless, but not since he'd been a wild kid from a dysfunctional family. As a SEAL, he'd learned that staying safe depended on his training and his faith in his teammates. Since neither of those had ever let him down, being told to stay safe was a waste of breath.

He'd almost screwed that up today, though. So maybe the words were a good reminder of what his duty was on this mission.

Throughout the rest of the day, Violet and Anderson traded Nate back and forth. Anderson took advantage of his kid-free time to run diagnostics on the security system and cameras. Then he spent time outside doing security checks. He had to make those trips around the perimeter of the property look as though he were doing yard work, but that was easily accomplished. He watered the shrubs in front of the house while keeping an eye on the street. He patrolled the backyard with a bottle of weed killer in his hand. No one questioned him, because he looked just like any other suburban dad.

After his final check of the property that evening, which he disguised as drinking a beer on his back deck, he went into the house and set the security system.

"Nate went out fast tonight," Violet said when Anderson walked into the dining room. "I think he's still tired from yesterday, but I'll take it."

Anderson looked at the table. She'd pushed the intel aside and had a jigsaw puzzle started. He picked up the box lid to look at the image. It was an ocean scene with a stingray swimming through the center. The puzzle was almost entirely shades of blue, which would make it challenging.

"Care to join me?" she asked, pushing out the chair next to her.

"Sure," he said and took the offered seat. Working on the puzzle would help keep his hands and mind engaged.

"I've separated the edge pieces from the center ones." She gestured to a small pile in front of her. "I like to put the edge together first."

"I didn't know there was a method to this." The few times in his life he'd done a puzzle, he'd just dumped the pieces on the table and had at it.

"You bet there is," she said, snapping together a corner. "Why don't you flip all the other pieces over so they're face up?"

"Okay." He started on the task assigned to him. "Learn anything new from the intel?"

"Thinking about it," she said, not looking up. "It's got to percolate." She'd used that expression when they were in Moscow, and he thought it a peculiar one… but letting ideas brew in her head worked for her. "I'm pretty sure we're not any more unsafe here than elsewhere."

"Not sure that's comforting," he commented.

She shrugged. "The truth is someone's looking for us. We can run and hide, but it won't last forever."

He nodded. "We'll have to make a stand." He'd been thinking throughout the day about how that might work. He didn't want it to be there—or anywhere she and Nate might be in the crossfire.

"I'm hoping to avoid that. Making a stand with…" She didn't need to finish the sentence. Worry about Nate's welfare had prevented any of Anderson's plans from developing fully.

They worked in silence for a while, both of them putting pieces into place. First, they formed the stingray. After the main image was complete, that left the more challenging ocean pieces. Anderson watched Violet's concentration as she selected pieces from the box.

"You don't go by color," he said, suddenly realizing that she was only using the shapes of the pieces to determine where they went.

"It's all about patterns." She reached for another piece. "There are only so many different shapes."

Leave it to her to treat a jigsaw puzzle like analysis work. "So why did you have me turn the pieces right side up?" he asked.

"That was for you. I didn't want you to feel bad when I put in the majority of the pieces. I thought seeing the colors might help even the score."

"Competitive puzzle making?" He chuckled. "Never heard of it."

"Anything can be a competition if one has a worthy opponent." She lifted his hand from the table and put a piece where it had been. Before dropping his hand, she gave it a squeeze.

"I'm glad you see me as worthy." His tone was joking, but he did like the way she perceived him.

She looked up, her eyes warm. "You're one of the fiercest competitors I know, but you better show some hustle or I'm going to win."

"Are you counting how many pieces you've put in?"

"Four-oh… make that 407," she said as she added another piece, "which means I'm closing in on half of them."

The way he saw it, he had two choices. He could rush to put in a few pieces, or he could use a more strategic approach, such as distraction. One definitely had more appeal than the other. He put his arm around her waist and pulled her onto his lap, making her laugh.

"I know what you're up to," she said, but she didn't try to move away.

"Will it work?" He didn't much care if it did, since he was enjoying the feel of her so close to him. Wanting to touch her in this way had come as a surprise. The attraction between them simmered undeniably, but there was a softness to their interactions now he'd never known before.

"It might," she conceded, her fingers curled into his shirt, "but there's a flaw in your plan. While I'm here, you can't put any pieces in the puzzle."

"Neither can you," he pointed out.

"Really?" She half turned in his arms and snapped a piece in with a flourish. "What do you say to that?"

He pulled her tighter to him, taking her lips in a kiss that made him forget about the puzzle entirely. She looped her arms around his neck as the kiss deepened. He could have stayed like that forever, but eventually she leaned back.

"Maybe we should go to bed," she suggested in a husky voice.

He'd love nothing better than to take her to bed, but worries about their safety stopped him from agreeing. "I think I'll stay down here on the couch tonight."

Her face was instantly serious. "Why?"

"I need to be ready if anyone tries to get in." He'd run through what he would do to prevent a breach of the home, and he'd concluded his best line of defense was to be downstairs.

"I think we're safe for now," she said, repeating her assessment from earlier.

He shook his head. "You know as well as I do that we're vulnerable. As you said, only constant movement would keep us safe, and we can't do that." Not with a baby in tow, he didn't bother to add.

She dropped her head onto his shoulder. "You're probably right. I was just… hopeful."

"I'm not willing to risk either of you on hope." He'd never forgive himself if something happened to her or Nate on his watch.

She stayed with him for a few minutes more, just resting against him. And it felt… nice. Finally, she lifted her head and gave him a small smile. "No putting in puzzle pieces while I'm sleeping."

"I promise," he said and stood, gently putting her on her feet. He gave her one more kiss and waited until she went upstairs before doing a last security sweep of the house. It was his duty to make sure Violet and Nate came out of this unharmed. He'd never forgive himself otherwise.

13

———————

"Anderson!" Violet calling his name brought him out of a light sleep. Something wasn't right. He checked his surroundings and heard her call for him again, her voice fainter this time. He reached for the gun he'd left on the coffee table and charged up the stairs.

When he reached the top, he saw her sitting on the hall floor with her head tucked between her knees. Was she injured? He looked for blood, some sign that she'd been attacked.

"What's wrong?" he said, coming to a stop and dropping down in front of her.

"I'm light-headed and feel awful." She tilted her head up; her face was pale. "I can't reach Nate. Will you get him out of bed?"

"Of course, but first you." He shoved the gun in his waistband so he could put an arm behind her back and one under her knees and lift her from the floor.

"I can walk," she murmured weakly, but her head rested against his chest.

"I don't think so." He carried her into the master bedroom and set her down gently on the bed.

"It's probably just a virus," she said as she dropped her head onto the pillow. "Maybe if I sleep for a while, I'll feel better."

"You need to stay in this bed for the rest of the day," he said, keeping his tone gentle.

"Can't do that. Moms don't get sick days."

"This one does. Consider yourself off the clock," Anderson said. He heard Nate's babbling through the monitor. "Let me get him, and I'll be back to check on you. Don't move."

When he returned to her twenty minutes later, Violet was curled on her side, sound asleep. She looked delicate and fragile, which wasn't her norm, and his heart hurt at the sight. Overcome by tenderness, he leaned closer to kiss her forehead. Her skin felt dry and too warm.

He retreated from the room, thinking about what he could do to make her feel better. He was rarely sick himself, but he figured she'd need fluids and something to treat what seemed like a fever.

"Looks like we're going to the store, buddy," he said to Nate. Grocery shopping with a baby seemed a daunting task, but he could do it. He made sure Nate had on a fresh diaper, grabbed the bag Violet always carried for him, and headed to the car.

"Good morning," Kelly called. She was powerwalking down the sidewalk.

"Hello," he responded as he strapped Nate in his seat.

"Early-morning trip?" Her pace slowed.

As much as Anderson knew that her question came from friendliness, it still made him uncomfortable. He didn't like to reveal details about his and Violet's lives. He had to say something, though, since it looked odd that he was leaving with the baby so early in the morning.

"Violet's under the weather today," he explained. "We're going to get some supplies."

"I'm sorry to hear that." Her face was instantly filled with concern. "Is there anything I can do?"

"No, I've got it. Thanks," he remembered to add. Part of him wished he could ask her to watch Nate for him, but he wasn't about to hand his child to anyone he hadn't run a full background check on.

Anderson drove to the nearest store, singing loudly and off-key to keep Nate entertained. Once they arrived, he realized the boy was too small to be put in a shopping cart seat—he'd probably slide out a leg hole.

The problem made Anderson hesitate. How did other parents do this? He looked around, but no one else had a baby at the store.

"Going to have to figure this out," he muttered to Nate. After a minute of debate, Anderson opted to carry him, which limited his purchases. He managed to buy Tylenol and Gatorade and hoped that combination would make Violet feel better.

He wasn't gone long, but when he returned to the safe house, he found a small plastic container waiting on the front steps. He approached it cautiously and saw the contents were frozen. Unexpected packages were not usually good things in his world, but the attached note erased his concern.

Homemade chicken noodle soup—good for any illness. Take care.

He didn't have to guess who it was from. He made sure to smile and wave in the direction of Kelly's house, knowing that she'd be watching for his reaction to the gift.

"I guess it's nice to have people who care about you," he muttered as he got Nate, his purchases, and the soup through the front door. He put Nate in the playpen and dashed up the stairs to check on Violet. He was glad to see she was still asleep. Since he might have his hands full with Nate when she woke, he left a bottle of Gatorade and some pills on the nightstand for her.

When he went back down, Nate had fallen asleep in the playpen. Now what? Anderson put his hands on his hips and looked around. He was out of tasks, and there was nothing he could do to ease their situation. He couldn't hunt down the bad guy, he couldn't patch the data breach, and no one needed him at the moment.

There must be something. He checked the encrypted phone. No messages, which meant nothing had changed. Next, he looked at his personal phone. He had a missed call from Patrick, which must have come in while he was at the store.

It would be good to talk to someone on the outside, get a different perspective. Anderson was feeling a little lost. Like he wasn't as in control as he should be—a sensation he hated. Violet's illness was part of that, but everything about their predicament had him feeling more apprehensive than usual.

Since he didn't trust his own phone, he dialed Patrick's number on Wiffy and was glad when his longtime friend picked up.

"Hey, man, good to hear from you," Patrick said. "How's it going?"

Anderson brought him up to speed on what had happened since he and Violet arrived at the safe house. He stuck to the facts, skipping over anything personal.

"What's really got you so worried?" Patrick asked after listening in near silence.

Anderson hesitated for a second, but he should have known Patrick would sense he wasn't getting the whole story. With a sigh, he admitted the truth. "I'm afraid I won't be able to protect them."

"Violet and your son?"

"Yeah." Anderson had gotten used to the idea of having a son, but it hit home again when Patrick said the word. "Violet's been in this kind of situation before, but Nate…"

"Kids change everything," Patrick agreed. Patrick had recently made a lot of changes in his life. First he married, and then his six-year-old daughter had come to live with him and his new wife. "But the rewards are worth it."

"I don't know about that," Anderson said and immediately felt guilty when he looked at his son sleeping in the playpen. Parenting was more challenging than he'd imagined, but the kid was… Aw, hell, he didn't know what to say about his relationship with Nate. He just knew that he felt inadequate, and that was enough to frustrate him, to make him doubt. "What if I screw it up?"

"You can't think that way," Patrick said. "Hey, do you remember when we were at Boy Scout camp?"

Anderson had only gone to the camp one time, the summer he was eight. Camp cost money, so his parents refused the other years. They'd let him stay in the Boy Scouts until he was twelve, though, even if their motivation wasn't the same as most parents'. Scout meetings had been held twice a week and always included snacks. His mom and dad had seen it as childcare and a free meal. Even then, Anderson had understood their game *and* known to hide it. He'd never eaten more than the other boys and maintained the fiction that his parents were working and that was why they didn't attend any events with him.

"Not among my finer moments," Anderson said.

"What are you talking about? You led an expedition into the woods."

"I got us all lost." The ill-fated nighttime trek was to hunt ghosts, after listening to countless ghost stories told around the campfire. Spirits never frightened Anderson, because he'd learned early on that things in the physical realm were plenty scary. Other kids had been afraid, though. A kid named Bobby had clung to him and cried, howling that they were all going to die.

"Yeah," Patrick said, "but you also got us back to camp. We panicked. You didn't."

"I got my ass chewed out," Anderson said. The camp counselors hadn't been happy with him, but to the other kids, he'd been a hero. At least for a day or two.

"They had to do that so other kids didn't wander off," Patrick said, "but they were proud of you, too. I heard them talking about it. You surprised them by staying calm and taking control."

"What's your point, Patrick?" Anderson demanded, tired of the trip down memory lane.

"You know what my point is," Patrick said. "You've got the right stuff in you to deal with any problems. Keep your cool, use your brain, and you'll be all right."

Anderson didn't know what to say. He wasn't used to getting pep talks from his buddies. Usually, talks like that weren't necessary. He knew his capabilities. With his SEAL team, everyone understood their roles and performed them. But this situation was different from any he'd been in before. It involved a child that was his and a woman he cared about more than he should.

"Thanks. I'll call you with updates," Anderson said and ended the call before Patrick could say more. His buddy had made it sound simple, but Anderson's problems were well beyond simple. "Aren't they, buddy?" he asked Nate as he looked into the playpen where the child stared up at him.

Nate pointed both index fingers toward Anderson and then fisted his hand and moved them toward himself. Wait a minute. That looked a lot like the sign for "come." Was it a fluke? Just an incidental movement? Anderson had shown Nate that sign and even used it with him several times, but had the baby picked it up for real? Anderson waited and watched. A few seconds later, Nate repeated the gesture.

"You got it." Anderson leaned closer and was rewarded with a huge baby smile that melted his heart. Why did the kid have to do that? Anderson didn't know, but he couldn't resist it either. He picked Nate up and got a pat on each cheek. "Do you mean kiss? It's supposed to be on your face, not mine, but I get your point."

For the first time, Anderson kissed his son's face. He'd seen Violet do it frequently, but he'd held back. But it was just the two of them now. No one to see. He pressed his lips to the boy's cheeks, surprised at their softness and the baby smell that came from him. Anderson knew it was just the scent of shampoo, but there was something special about it.

"Okay, now what are we going to do, because we can't bother Mama today. We probably should check on her, though. Promise to be quiet." Anderson carried Nate up to the bedroom and peeked in. Violet must have woken at some point, because the Tylenol and half the bottle of Gatorade were gone. That was a good sign. With the rest she was getting, he hoped she'd recover quickly.

"New diaper for you," he said to Nate after they crept out of Violet's room, "and then... something."

Anderson spent the next hour keeping Nate happy. They went to the windows, looking for birds and butterflies. Then Anderson dug through the basket of toys in the living room. Nothing lasted for more than a few minutes before Nate tossed it aside, seemingly dissatisfied. When he started to fuss, Anderson looked around, desperate for a solution, and spotted the carrier that Violet sometimes used. He adjusted the straps to fit him and put Nate in so the boy was chest to chest with him. The baby was instantly soothed.

"Good deal," Anderson said, "and my hands are free." He paced the house looking for little tasks he could do. He jotted some notes in his notebook, all the while telling Nate what he was writing. The sound of his voice helped keep Nate happy. In the kitchen, Anderson reorganized the pantry and the refrigerator, arranging like items together.

He was idly putting puzzle pieces in place and telling Nate that his mama was going to be mad about him working on the puzzle without her when he realized that Nate had fallen asleep against him.

"Finally out, huh?" Anderson asked softly and smoothed a hand over Nate's head. Carefully, Anderson took off the carrier and got Nate out. He knew that he should put his son in the playpen or his crib for a nap, but there was something about holding the boy that captivated him. He'd learned lots about kids recently, and one of those things was that sleeping babies were perfect little works of art.

He'd just sit with him on the couch for a few minutes before putting him down. Anderson reclined on the sofa with Nate resting on his chest and felt an unexpected contentment come over him.

14

———

Violet opened her eyes, feeling like a truck had slammed into her. She'd spent the entire day before in bed, only waking a few times when Anderson came to check on her. She'd heard Nate cry just once, so Anderson must have kept the baby entertained.

She was lucky Anderson was there. He'd cared for her in a way that suggested there might be more between them than attraction. She'd felt him tuck the blankets around her, stroke her hair, and kiss her forehead. She'd seen the same gentleness in the way he acted with Nate. Could it be that he wanted to be a family?

She shouldn't let herself hope, since it might only lead to disappointment. But during their time together, she'd realized that her interest in him was deeper than she'd initially thought. Maybe it was sharing a child with him that brought on these feelings, but she wanted him in her life. Staring at the ceiling, she let out a long sigh.

Slowly, she got out of bed and put on fresh clothes. In the bathroom, she brushed her teeth and slathered tinted moisturizer on her face to improve her wan appearance. She eyed herself in the mirror. She looked almost human—not good, but alive and functioning. When she was dressed, she made her way down the stairs, keeping a hand on the rail.

"What are you doing out of bed?" Anderson strode up the stairs to meet her before she got more than halfway down.

"I'm better. I think," she said, still feeling light-headed. "Thanks for taking over yesterday."

"No problem." He was studying her face closely. "You need to spend the day on the couch."

He put his arm around her waist and guided her into the living room, where he settled her on the couch and even propped a pillow behind her back. She glanced up into his concerned face, trying to see past it to his heart. If she could see inside him, what would she find? A man just doing what he had to to see this mission through? Or something else, something more personal.

"Thanks," she murmured, managing a slight smile.

"What can I get you?" he asked.

"Nothing." She hated to admit that just doing what she had left her feeling shaky. Her legs were wobbly, and she felt clammy all over. Maybe a day on the couch was a good plan. "Where's Nate?"

"Snoozing in his crib," Anderson said.

"Oh, that's unusual at this time." She glanced at the clock. Nate's schedule had been a little off since moving to the safe house, but this was way out of whack. "Did he get up early?"

"No, he just seemed tired, so I put him down."

She nodded, having no choice but to defer to Anderson's judgment since she hadn't been there to evaluate Nate for herself. It was probably fine.

"Would you like me to bring you the intel?" Anderson offered. It was still in the dining room, which seemed a long way off considering how she felt.

"Sure, that'll give me something to do," she said.

Anderson retrieved various folders and the laptop. She reviewed everything that she'd already looked at, but nothing new popped out at her. It was frustrating. She had to be missing some detail that revealed why they were being targeted and by whom precisely. Signs pointed to Volkhov's organization, but she couldn't be sure who was pursuing them on his behalf. If she could be certain of that, they might be able to take action and end it. Not knowing was driving her up the wall.

She tossed the folder she'd been reviewing onto the coffee table and listened for Anderson and Nate. Babbling sounds from the kitchen told her where they were, so she got up, determined to join them. She made it to the kitchen doorway and leaned against the jamb. Anderson had Nate in the baby carrier and was emptying the dishwasher. Instead of bending over to retrieve the dishes, Anderson was doing squats and powering up. The motion made Nate squeal every time.

"Are you sure you should do that with him?" she asked. In her imagination, she saw Nate fly out the top of the carrier and crash to the floor.

Anderson stilled at her words. "It seems okay," he said, "but if you prefer I didn't, I'll stop."

"Please," she said. "I don't think it's safe." Her fears were probably unfounded, but she couldn't keep from worrying.

"Sure," Anderson agreed readily. "We're headed to the backyard for a bit. Do you want to sit on the deck?"

A leftover wave of dizziness came over her, and she shook her head. "Remember to keep him out of direct sun. Baby skin burns so easily."

"Do you have sunscreen for him?"

"No," she snapped, "you can't use that on babies his age." How did Anderson not know that? "You can't put chemicals on young skin."

"Right," Anderson said, his expression going flat. "I didn't realize that."

"I'm going back to the couch," she said, since her head was spinning a bit.

"Can I get you anything?" Anderson asked. "Toast, crackers?"

She mumbled a "No, thanks" and returned to the couch, where she fell asleep. When she woke, it was early evening and she felt better. The room didn't move when she sat up. That was an improvement. She glanced around the space. Nate must have been playing in the living room while she slept. Toys, usually kept in the basket, were scattered across the floor. She felt instant guilt. She should have known her son was playing just feet away from her, but she'd slept through it. How could she relinquish the care of her child to a man who knew almost nothing about kids?

Anderson had done fine, she reminded herself—but he was inexperienced. And what if something had happened? Did Anderson know CPR for infants? Was he aware of choking hazards? He was trained for battlefield wounds, not kid stuff. What if…

She stopped herself. She was being irrational. Anderson was an intelligent man. He'd make an appropriate decision. Hell, he could simply have woken her up if he needed help. But as much as she might be interested in a relationship with Anderson, she could never forget that Nate was ultimately her responsibility. She'd accepted that when she read the plus sign on the pregnancy test. And that made it tough to relinquish control. Tough to deal with being on the run, hunted.

She was just worn down, that was the problem. Worn down and frustrated with their situation. She eyed the intel that still sat on the coffee table and grimaced. Just as she reached for it to take another look, she heard water running in the bathtub overhead.

Anderson had helped with Nate's bath, but he'd never done the entire thing. Did he know the correct water temperature? Did he know not to leave Nate in the tub unattended for even a second?

She got off the couch more quickly than she'd moved in two days. Upstairs, she opened the bathroom door. Nate was in the tub by himself with Anderson's large hand supporting his back. They were both laughing, but it didn't reduce her stress. Nate could easily fall over, and a baby could drown in just an inch of water.

"You shouldn't bathe him that way," she said. "He's not stable sitting up yet."

"I've got him, Violet. He's not going anywhere." Anderson wrung out the washcloth one-handed and draped it over the side of the tub.

"He could slip away from you so easily." Kids were notoriously difficult to hang onto.

Anderson sighed. "I'll take him out, since we're done anyway. Do you want to put him to bed?"

"I…" She didn't yet trust herself to carry Nate. "Will you take him to his room? I can get it from there." She managed to dress Nate in a sleeper and lift him into his crib. Wanting to spend some time with him, she stayed, stroked his hair, and sang a lullaby until he fell asleep. She had to admit that he appeared to be just fine after two days of Anderson's care, but her mother's heart felt heavy.

When she made her way back downstairs, Anderson was coming from the kitchen with a half-drunk beer in his hand. He followed her into the living room, where she dropped to the floor and began gathering up the scattered toys to return them to the basket. When she finished, she looked up to see him silently watching her.

"I suppose I did that wrong, too," he said as he took a swallow of beer.

"Huh?" What was he talking about?

"I didn't pick up the toys right away, didn't know about sunscreen, gave him his bath wrong. Anything else I screwed up today?" he demanded.

"What are you—"

"I told you from the beginning that I'm not cut out to be a parent." He slammed the beer bottle down on the coffee table. "I guess I've proven that to you now."

"That's not… I didn't mean to nitpick. It's just—"

He shot her a look that made her stop speaking. "You don't trust me to care for him, and I guess I can't blame you there, since you know me and my family history."

She knew what her research had told her and what he himself had said a few evenings earlier. He had real concerns about his ability to parent, but she thought she'd reassured him about that. Except… except today, when she'd undercut that reassurance with every word she'd said to him. She'd done nothing but criticize. Sinking down on the couch, she dropped her head in her hands.

"I understand you want what's best for Nate and feel the need to be in charge of his care." Anderson's tone was carefully neutral. "That's your right as his mother, and you do it well. We both need to accept that I can't be a dad. It's not in me."

"I'm sorry," she said, looking up. "I didn't mean for it to come off like that. I'm just... the stress is getting to me. I was doing okay until I got sick, and then..." She was making excuses, which she hated, but there was some truth to them as well. She was frustrated by their helplessness, frustrated by their predicament, and frustrated with herself for not being able to do more. "You stepped up and cared for him. You did what a dad does. So well. Please don't say you aren't capable of being a father to Nate, because it's just not true."

"It *is* true," he countered. "Being a mom comes so naturally to you. You're amazing at it, and from what you've said, you had a great example. That's how this works, so it makes sense that you've got it all together."

"Thanks," she said. "I appreciate that." His compliment meant a lot to her, and she smiled at him. He didn't return the expression. If anything, he looked more upset, lips pursed and brow wrinkled. What was that about? She straightened the folders on the coffee table and tried to analyze his mood.

Oh. The light bulb went on for her a second later. By accepting his compliment that she was a good mother from a line of good mothers, she'd just reinforced his belief that *he* couldn't be a good father since he'd had no example.

She caught movement out of the corner of her eye and saw Anderson headed from the room.

"Anderson. Wait. Please come back. I need to tell you something," she said, making up her mind to share details with him that she'd only told her mother.

"What?" His tone was flat, which made it more difficult for her to continue.

She had to tell him, though. She owed him that, and she was glad when he came back and sat in a chair facing her. It still took her a few seconds to begin.

"I've told you that I refused to acknowledge that I was pregnant until it was undeniable. What I didn't tell you was the complete panic I felt. I didn't think I could do it." She remembered her racing heartbeat and how she'd sat on the bathroom floor for an hour, filled with terror. Afterward she'd managed to drag herself into her bedroom, where she'd sprawled across the bed, staring at the ceiling in paralyzed fear.

"By yourself, you mean," he said, misinterpreting her words.

"I didn't think I could be a mom at all." She had to make him understand this. Finding out she was going to have a baby had been the most emotionally chaotic time of her life. Joy and fear mixed together. "I didn't think I was good enough to be entrusted with a baby. Me? Seriously? What twist of fate would make me a parent?"

"What are you talking about?" His eyes narrowed. "You're intelligent and talented. You've got more going for you than a lot of people."

"In those realms, maybe, but the ability to love and care for a child… that's way different. I was so afraid I couldn't do it. I worried throughout my pregnancy, and when he was born…" She paused to gather her thoughts. "I looked at him, and he was so beautiful and perfect that I didn't feel I could be trusted to care for him. I knew nothing about babies."

"Your mom was there," he said, making her wonder if she was reaching him. "You told me that."

"She was and thank God for that, but he was *mine*. And I'm still learning how to care for him one day at a time. I've read a million books, listened to podcasts, and taken advice from people I trust. And that all has helped…" and here was what she needed Anderson to see, "but what I figured out late one night when Nate was about a month old was that all it took was love. I loved him so completely that I knew I could make it work. I could be the mom he needs and deserves. I'm still scared sometimes, though. I question if I'm doing things right every day. I think every parent must do that."

He said nothing when she finished speaking. After a minute, he gave a brief nod and left the room. She could only hope her words about raising a child with love had reached him. Anderson had love inside him. She'd seen the way he'd interacted with Nate, the way he'd held her and loved her. It was there… but he had to let himself feel it.

15

"Shush, baby, it's okay," Violet whispered to Nate, trying to calm the fussy boy. He'd woken three times in the night. Twice she'd gotten to him first, but Anderson had settled him at four that morning, rocking Nate gently until his eyes closed.

And Anderson insisted he was no good at being a father. She shook her head. That wasn't what she'd seen during the night or for any of the time they'd been on the run. He was inexperienced, but he seemed to innately get what to do.

"He's a good daddy, isn't he?" She moved Nate to the changing table and began dressing him for the day. "He just doesn't know it yet."

She'd worried throughout the sleepless and lonely night that her words hadn't been enough to convince Anderson that he could do this. She'd admitted her own fears in the hope he'd see that no one had it all together. Parenting wasn't something that came easily. Her own mother referred to it as the toughest job anyone had ever done. Violet couldn't argue with that assessment.

"People who claim this is easy are foolish," she said to Nate in a singsong voice, "Or they're actors on television shows where everything is perfect." Nate giggled at her tone of voice. "That's right," she continued, "those people are silly." She slipped a clean shirt over the baby's head. "But what are we going to do about your daddy?"

"We need to pack," Anderson said from the doorway.

She stiffened. How long had he been standing there? Had he heard what she'd said to Nate? Oh, God, she didn't want to reopen that conversation. Not now.

"Did something happen?" she asked, choosing to shift away from the personal. There would be a time when she'd pour out her heart to him, but it wasn't then.

"No developments," he said, "but they've located a different safe house for us and given me coordinates to pick up new IDs."

She noticed the smile that came to Nate's face at the sound of Anderson's voice. The boy was becoming attached to his father. He was going to be upset if they were separated.

"We're moving today?" That was more sudden than she'd anticipated. Rogers's team was certainly efficient. She guessed she should be grateful, but the thought of moving wasn't fun. Violet glanced around the room. In her shopping trips, she'd acquired several things for Nate that she didn't want to leave behind. Clothes, toys, a playpen, and a bouncy seat.

"Looks like it. I'll gather stuff up downstairs."

"I've got this," she said, but Anderson was already walking away. Nate let out a whimper when Anderson left. "I know, baby. I didn't want him to go either."

Over the next half hour, she alternately carried Nate on her hip as she packed up his room and put him down in his crib. He'd lie content for only a few minutes at a time, making her task more difficult.

Her belongings took much less time to gather, but Nate wasn't willing to lie on her bed long enough for her to even put her few items of clothing and cosmetics in a bag. By the time she took him downstairs, she felt frazzled and overwrought. She'd been in tough spots before, but never with a child dependent on her.

The truth was that she wanted this to be over so she could take Nate home, even if she had to do it alone. She didn't like thinking about that possibility, but she acknowledged that the uncertainty between her and Anderson added a layer of stress she didn't need.

"Come on." She adjusted Nate against her, picked up her bag, and took one last sweep of the room before going downstairs. When she reached the bottom step, Anderson held out the files that they'd picked up days earlier.

"You need to take another look at these," he said without preamble. "It's possible you missed something. You've got an hour before we need to leave." His tone was all business, making her wonder if anything she'd said to him the evening before had sunk in. Would he even give them a chance as a family?

She swallowed and closed her eyes for a minute to gather her strength. None of this was what she needed after two days of being sick, and a night with a fussy baby. And she was irritated about Anderson's directive. She'd combed through those pages, made notes, let it sift around in her brain, and nothing had clicked. Because there *was* nothing, she'd concluded. Hearing that she hadn't done a good enough job made her feel useless. Normally, she was okay with criticism, but this wasn't the morning for it.

She wanted a minute to herself, a chance to think. She was struggling to hold in the overwhelmed feeling when Nate's little fist gripped the collar of her shirt, bunching it up as his fingernails scraped against her skin.

"Ouch, baby," she said, gently prying his hand loose. She felt hot tears come to her eyes and tried to blink them back.

"Did he hurt you?" Anderson asked, dropping the files and taking Nate from her.

"No, it's not him. I'm just…" She drew in a breath, trying to steady herself. This was no time to have a breakdown.

"What is it, then?" Anderson put his arm around her shoulders and led her to the living room to sit.

He didn't understand, but at least he was trying to be nice. She appreciated that, but somehow his sudden kindness brought the tears on faster. She hadn't been such an emotional wreck since the weeks after Nate's birth when she'd been on a hormonal roller-coaster.

"Nothing. It's fine. I'm fine." She brushed away the tears and tried to force others back.

Anderson's eyes were on her as he bounced Nate on his knee. After a minute, he said, "Violet, you don't have to fake having it all together in front of me. I heard what you said last night about struggling to be a good mom."

She gave him a small smile and admitted the truth. "It's hard to do it all."

"But you're doing it," he said. "You're caring for Nate. You're the smartest analyst I've ever worked with. Seriously, Violet, you're an amazing woman."

"Thanks," she said, but she didn't want a personal cheerleader. He meant well, she got that. "I just need a minute." She focused on her clasped hands and slowly drew in several breaths. In the background, she realized Anderson and Nate had quietly left the room.

It would have been a good time for a long run or a yoga session, but she didn't have the opportunity for either of those things. The best she could hope for was ten minutes to pull herself together and deal with the feeling of being overwhelmed by her responsibilities.

After several slow breaths in, she started to get things in perspective, and the sense that she was going to fall apart retreated until it was only a haze at the edges of her vision. It didn't disappear, but she could keep it at bay for a little longer. Until they got out of this situation. With one last breath in, she pushed herself off the couch. No more sitting around, she told herself. She had work to do and a family to move.

An hour later, they were ready to change houses. She'd taken a look at the pages indicated by Rogers's team, but she still couldn't see that she'd missed something that would shed light on their problem. She'd try again later when they were someplace safe.

"I'm finished," she called to Anderson, who was holding Nate and doing one more sweep through the upstairs to make sure they hadn't forgotten anything. "I'm going to put a few things in the car."

She opened the front door and stopped dead. A black SUV sat at the curb and another blocked the end of their driveway. She retreated immediately, slamming the door closed. So stupid, she cursed herself. She hadn't checked her surroundings before leaving the house. It was a rookie mistake, and now whoever was out there would know they'd been seen. They would act quickly.

"What is it?" Anderson questioned, suddenly beside her. He must have sensed the danger, because he dragged her to the floor with him.

"Where's Nate?" She felt icy hands around her heart at the thought of putting Nate in jeopardy.

"In his crib. I heard you slam the door." Anderson was pulling a gun from his waistband. "How many?"

"Two vehicles. I didn't see any men"—she replayed the scene in front of the house in her mind—"but they have to be out there."

Anderson slid on his stomach to a tactical bag near the door, removed an additional handgun, and gave it to her. "Take this and go upstairs. If they get past me, you know what to do."

She'd had defensive training and went to the range regularly as part of her job. She'd used the skills more than once while on a mission, but she'd never had so much at stake before.

Anderson inched his way closer to the window. Before he reached it, the sound of the back door splintering cut through the air. "Go," he said to her in an urgent whisper as he rose to a crouch, but she couldn't let him face what might be several unknown assailants alone.

"I'll give you backup." She retreated to the foot of the stairs but held her ground there.

He shot her an irritated look and shook his head as he moved quietly toward the kitchen. A large man in black tactical gear rounded the corner and nearly collided with Anderson. Anderson punched the man in the throat, making him drop to the floor. Violet scrambled forward, taking handcuffs from the man's belt and snapping them on his wrists.

"Upstairs," Anderson mouthed at her, but she shook her head.

Two more assailants entered the room. Anderson brought one down with a sharp right to the jaw, but the other lunged past him, headed for Violet and the stairs.

"I wouldn't," she said, taking aim at the man's chest. Before she had to make the decision to pull the trigger, Anderson put a sleeper hold on the man, quickly rendering him unconscious.

"How many?" Anderson growled in the ear of the handcuffed man. When the man didn't answer, he asked again in Russian. Anderson's grip was white knuckled around the man's throat as he lifted him from the ground.

The assailant gasped out an answer that Violet couldn't hear, but Anderson held up a finger to indicate one more before sliding out of the room. Ten seconds later, she heard a grunt and a thump as a heavy body went down.

"Got him," Anderson said softly as he re-entered the room. "I'm going to check around. You okay?"

She gave a single nod before helping Anderson handcuff the remaining assailants. Inside, she was shaking. She'd never come close to shooting someone. She'd faced danger and had to fight in the past, but never had she held a gun on another human. It left her unnerved.

When she heard Nate's soft whimper, she glanced up the stairs. He might be scared at the strange noises. Soundlessly, she took the steps, knowing that Anderson would handle everything else.

She was sitting in the rocker, a gun wedged alongside her, when Anderson came to the nursery a few minutes later.

"No one else," he said, reaching for her gun and ejecting the magazine. "I called Rogers's team." He set the gun aside and reached out to stroke Nate's hair. "They're on their way, along with the local police."

"That'll give the neighbors a show," she said, imagining the gossip that would fly up and down the street.

Anderson chuckled, and some of her tension eased. He shifted his hand from Nate's head to her cheek and tucked a lock of hair that had come loose from her ponytail behind her ear. "You scared me down there."

"I'm trained, you know." She tried to smile at him.

"I know, but I still don't want you in a firefight."

She wanted to ask his meaning. Did he feel that way because of her, what she meant to him, or simply because she was the mother of their child? She wasn't brave enough to ask, and a sudden thought sent a shiver through her. The bad guys had been caught. The circumstances that forced them together were over, which meant she and Anderson could go their separate ways. Was that what would happen now? Or had something worth pursuing come out of it? She was convinced it had—but was he?

She studied Anderson's face, trying to read his thoughts, but he revealed nothing.

"I'm going to go meet Rogers's guys," he said. "They probably have a plan to keep this quiet, since this is one of their safe houses."

"Sure," she agreed, knowing it was best if she didn't try to talk about their relationship while Anderson was still in protective mode. It would wait a little longer.

She watched from upstairs as Allen Zimmerman and three other members of Rogers's team entered from the back alley to manage the situation. No doubt they were keeping it as low key as possible. Two police squad cars parked in the street were the only indications of a problem. Violet saw Jeff, Kelly, Evie, and several other people from the neighborhood standing across the street, but the most they got to see was one man put in the back of a police car and driven off. She guessed that had been done for show. The other assailants were taken out the back way.

16

———

"What did you tell Jeff?" Violet asked when she took Nate downstairs after the police left. She'd seen their neighbor cross the lawn between the houses and knock on the door, but she hadn't been able to overhear Anderson's conversation with him.

"Random home invasion," he said, "but the police are investigating a possible link between the perp and this house."

"He bought that?" It didn't seem likely to her. "What about the two SUVs outside?"

"A couple of Rogers's guys drove off in them. No one asked any questions."

"Do you think the neighbors are that gullible?"

He shrugged. "Does it matter?"

She supposed not, but she liked the neighbors, even if they were a bit nosy. It was nice to know people cared about them.

"I was going to make an omelet for dinner. Want to join me?" Anderson said.

"I'd like that." She followed him to the kitchen, put Nate in his high chair, and opened a jar of baby food for him. "Yummy apricots," she said as she tried to coax him to open his mouth for the plastic spoon. Eating this way was new to Nate, but she'd had some success.

"When can he eat actual people food?" Anderson asked as he broke eggs into a bowl. He'd surprised her in the time they'd lived together with his ability to cook. It wasn't gourmet food, but it tasted good and she was thankful for his skills.

"A few more months yet, according to his pediatrician." She wiped apricot puree from Nate's face and tried to spoon more into his mouth. She was aware of Anderson working at the stove, but her mind kept wandering to the assailants. Something wasn't adding up in her head. The guys didn't quite fit the profile she'd worked up.

A few minutes later, Anderson slid a plate in front of her. "Vegetable omelet. Just the way you like it. No meat, a little cheese."

"Thanks," she said, picking up her fork and noticing that cheese and ham oozed from the side of Anderson's omelet. She sliced into her meal and ate slowly while her brain sorted out what had happened that afternoon. Across the table, she was aware of Anderson talking to Nate and occasionally spooning more apricots into the boy's mouth.

"What is it?" Anderson asked after several minutes of silence.

"Huh?" She blinked and focused on him.

"Your mind's somewhere else. You get that look when you're letting intel percolate."

He would notice, she thought. Talking it out with him might help. "Did it seem to you that you took out those four guys a little too easily?"

"I wasn't working alone," he pointed out.

"I didn't do much." She'd held a gun on one, giving Anderson the opportunity to deal with another assailant.

"Just say it," he said, making her look up and meet his eyes.

"I'm not insulting your manliness or training." She didn't want him to take offense. She knew he was more than capable of disarming four guys by himself, but the speed and ease with which it had all been done left her wondering.

"And I wasn't taking it that way."

"Okay," she said, putting her thoughts into words. "If those guys were Russian mob executioners, Volkhov's men or otherwise, they went down too fast." She tapped her fingers against the table. "We've dealt with that breed before. Can you imagine any of the executioners we encountered in Moscow being taken out in less time than it takes me to change Nate's diaper? And why attack in broad daylight? And if they're going to be so bold, why weren't their guns even drawn as they entered the house? And why were there four at all? We thought it was a single enemy."

"That's a lot of questions." His tone was cautious and a little doubtful.

"I've got more if you want to hear them." An infinite number of questions crowded for space in her head, so many that she was struggling to sort them into categories.

"I don't," he said abruptly. "Let's accept that it's over. That's what Rogers's guys think, and they tend to be right."

So did she, she wanted to argue. She'd never made an inaccurate prediction that she knew of. Her suggestions hadn't always been followed by her superiors, but she had a track record of being spot on. She'd gotten lucky one time, she acknowledged. She'd made the correct prediction, but it was based on incorrect data. If she'd had the right intel, her advice would have been very different. It had shaken her confidence—but, ironically, gotten her a promotion.

She struggled to shake off her unease about their current situation. Something nagged at her.

Yet she wanted it to be over. Living with the threat of constant danger had worn on her nerves. Maybe that's all her questions were: her own unwillingness to let her guard down. She'd been in a state of high alert since her car was riddled with bullets, and it was tough to let it go.

"Maybe you're right," she conceded, accepting that stress and adrenaline might be driving her thoughts more than logic and facts were. Her worries were still spinning around in her head, but she'd review the intel again in the morning when she'd rested and could think more clearly. They could put Nate to bed, snuggle on the couch, and watch a movie. That sounded like the perfect way to end the chaos of the day. She was just about to suggest it when he spoke.

"I need to make some phone calls so I can figure out how to get the hell out of here." He sounded desperate to leave, a man formulating an escape route.

She turned her attention to him, truly looking at his face for the first time in several minutes. The tension that should have left when the bad guys were hauled away was still there. It might even be stronger. But what was the source, since he seemed to accept that the Russian mob was no longer after them?

"We'll need separate cars to get home. I can pick mine up where it's being held, but you don't own one at all anymore. Rogers can probably help you out with that. I won't leave until I know you have a way home." He ticked off details as if planning a mission.

He'd moved on, she realized, catching on to his train of thought. He was worried about how they could go their separate ways. So it *was* over between them. That's what he was saying. She picked up her water glass and forced herself to take a swallow while she tried to formulate a response.

"I heard from my CO earlier today," he continued. "There's a mission deploying in two weeks that he wants me on, so I have just enough time to go home and close up my house before I need to be back on base."

"And after that?" she asked, proud of her calm tone.

"There'll be another mission. Always is." He met her eyes over the table. "I'm never in the States for more than a few weeks at a time."

That might have been true for him, though she knew other SEALs who weren't deployed as often. Anderson had language skills that made him unique, but she suspected he volunteered for extra duties. Either way, his message to her was clear. He wasn't interested in being a dad to Nate or anything to her.

She stood up. "Can we talk about this in the morning? I'm tired, and you must be, too. Let's make it an early night." She detached the tray from Nate's high chair and lifted him out.

"That's a good idea," he said. "I'll stay down here on the couch."

"Why would you do that, since you think the danger is over?" she asked, though she knew the answer she would receive. He didn't want to share a bed with her. Hell, he didn't want to sleep on the same floor of the house, apparently.

"You know why, Violet," he said, taking Nate from her. "I'll settle him for the night. You go to bed." He walked out of the kitchen ahead of her and headed for the stairs.

She'd never been ordered to bed by a man, and everything in her bristled against it. He was dismissing her as if she were a child, which hurt, but the worst part was that he was dismissing Nate as well. And that broke her heart.

She stood in the kitchen listening to the sounds overhead. Anderson was talking to Nate as he got him ready for bed—as if he wasn't going to walk away from his son tomorrow. How could he do that? No matter what Anderson believed about himself as a potential father, didn't he have some affection for the child he'd helped care for?

Anger and sorrow rose in Violet in equal amounts, and she knew she wasn't going to be able to stay silent. She gathered up their dinner dishes, loaded the dishwasher, and cleaned the kitchen while she waited for Anderson to come back down. When her tasks were done, she paced around the living room until she heard footsteps on the stairs. She whirled to face him.

"I thought you were going to bed," Anderson said, tossing a blanket and a pillow on the couch.

"And I thought you might care about Nate and me," she shot back.

"I do," he said, scrubbing a hand over his face, "but it's… complicated."

"What's complicated about it? Across the world there are millions of families where this isn't complicated." She worked to calm her tone.

"Right. Millions of normal families from generations of normal families, who know how to be a family. We don't." His hands went to his hips.

They *were* a family, but insisting on that wasn't the right tack with him. "Do you think all those *normal* moms and dads instinctively knew how to be parents? I'm sure they didn't. The fact that you seem to think you aren't fatherly shouldn't prevent you from trying."

"I can't do it, Violet," he declared. "I never said I would. In fact, I clearly told you the opposite."

"You don't love him, then?" She watched his face closely, watched his eyes shift as he tried to formulate an answer to her question. He didn't want to respond. That was obvious. But why? Because he didn't love his son… or was it something else? Was it about her?

He turned away and arranged the blanket on the couch, carefully tucking it in as if doing that tucked away his emotions as well. It was neat and compartmentalized, and she felt like tearing it apart. She had the overwhelming sense that this was her last opportunity to reach him. In the morning, he'd find excuses not to discuss their relationship and probably have her packed into a new car and sent home by noon. This was the time to be honest about her own feelings toward him, because she might not get another chance.

"Anderson, look at me." She waited until he turned toward her. His arms went across his chest in a defensive posture, but he wasn't going to deter her from what she had to say. "I want us to be a family, for Nate's sake. Every little boy should have a daddy, and despite what you say, I think you love him. I know you'd do anything to protect him and make sure he had what he needed—and those are behaviors of a loving father. I'm done with hearing that you aren't father material because you had a lousy dad yourself." His eyes narrowed, dark and dangerous. "I'd think you'd want to prove you could be a good dad despite that."

"Don't goad me," he warned. She almost smiled at him. His words reminded her of their exchanges in Moscow when the white heat of their attraction had flared. She'd missed the banter later, but she'd also come to realize how much she'd misunderstood their initial relationship. What had happened halfway around the world had formed the basis of what they had now. If she could only make him see that.

"I'm not," she said. "I'm speaking the truth, and you know it—but I'm not done yet." She paused for a few seconds to gather her strength before plunging on. "Sometime, somehow, I fell in love with you. It started during our fights in Russia, and it's what drove me to seek you out and tell you we had a son." It was only as she made that declaration that she realized it was true—that love for him had been her impetus. She'd thought it only fair that he know of their child, but somewhere deep inside her she'd clung to the hope of love with Anderson. She'd lied to herself about the strength of her feelings for Anderson, but she wasn't doing that anymore. "And the time here has made me sure of my love for you. I want you in my life, Anderson—for Nate, but for me, too."

She could have gone on detailing the reasons she loved him, the ways she loved him, but she could see he was struggling. His jaw was hard set, as if working to keep something in… or keep love out. She didn't know which, so she waited, hoping that she'd gotten through to him.

"Go to bed, Violet," he finally said, repeating his command from an hour earlier.

"You have nothing to say to me?" she asked softly. She wasn't expecting a declaration of love, but she'd hoped for something that showed she mattered to him.

"Just that I've fulfilled my end of the bargain." His words seemed rationed out. "I've protected you and Nate. You're safe now, and this is over. I'll make sure you get home, and I'll arrange financial support for Nate. That's it, Violet." He held his hands out in the "all gone" gesture she'd seen him use with Nate. "That's all I've got to give."

She felt her face crack, fracture into a thousand pieces, and found herself unable to speak. As she went past him to the stairs, she didn't know if she felt more hurt for herself or for him. If he truly believed he had nothing to give her and Nate, that was the saddest thing she'd ever heard.

17

Violet struggled up out of nightmares when her phone's alarm went off. Nate would be waking any minute for his morning feeding. If she got out of bed that instant, she could at least brush her teeth before going to him. Instead, she remained under the covers. Clean teeth weren't enough motivation to make her move yet. It had taken her hours to get to even a fitful sleep. She'd replayed her conversation with Anderson a hundred times in her head.

On the one hand, she was proud of what she'd managed to say. She'd laid it on the line, and that had felt good… in a way. Anderson's absolute unwillingness to even consider staying with her and Nate, though, left her with a crushing sensation in her chest. Once, during the night, she'd heard him come upstairs, and she'd had a fleeting hope he'd come to her, but he passed her room and went to Nate's. She'd watched the clock. Anderson had stayed in the boy's room for precisely ten minutes before she heard his footsteps going back down the stairs.

In the morning quiet, she listened for any movement from downstairs, but it was absolutely still. As far as she knew, he had already left. She could imagine him staying up throughout the night and making the arrangements. It would all be very neat and tidy, perfectly orchestrated, but the outcome would be that he was leaving her, leaving them.

Maybe he was simply out on a patrol of the neighborhood. He seemed to think it necessary to do that, even if this wasn't the most exciting place. Other days, he'd returned from his early-morning reconnaissance missions and told her funny stories. A man on the next street let his dog out in the yard and stood buck naked in the window waiting for the animal to come back in. A jogger who flailed like a windmill when she ran had nearly plowed Anderson over on a different morning.

She winced, recalling the domestic scenes in the kitchen while they made breakfast and planned their days. It had seemed so real to her, but if what he'd said the night before was true, he'd simply been doing a job.

Her phone screen glowed with a message. She scrambled for it, wanting it to be Anderson, but it was her mom.

Just checking on you and Nate. Love you.

Violet could have sent a message back, but the thought of hearing her mom's voice was too great a temptation—and besides, she should tell her mom that they were safe. She hit the call button.

"Good morning, sweetie," her mom said immediately.

"Hi, Mom. I wanted to let you know that Nate and I'll be going home soon, probably today. The situation is over, and we're fine." She didn't give the details of the home invasion. No need to worry her mom now that it was over.

"I'm so relieved to hear that. Would you mind if I come for a visit soon?"

"Not at all. Nate and I would love to see you." The thought of some time with her mom made Violet feel marginally better.

"Are you going home alone?" Her mother's voice softened.

"Looks like it. Anderson's not interested in being a father." There, she'd made herself say that.

"His loss." Her mom's reply made her smile a little. "But yours and Nate's, too. I'm sorry, sweetie."

"Me, too. I had hoped… Well, I shouldn't be surprised. My analysis, you know. Oh, Mom, I wanted to be wrong about him. And I've made another terrible— Just a second." She thought she heard a sound, so she paused and listened for Nate. When it wasn't repeated, she went on and told her mother about her conversation with Anderson the night before. "I told him I loved him and wanted a life with him, and he said that he had nothing to give. I took a giant risk and… miscalculated."

For someone who analyzed risk and made projections for a living, she hadn't seen her situation with Anderson very clearly.

"Maybe when he's away from you and Nate, he'll realize what he's missing," her mother suggested.

"I suppose that's possible," she said, but Anderson would be on a mission within the month and all his attention would be focused on the job. Would he even spare a thought for them?

A door downstairs opened and closed. He must be back from his neighborhood patrol. She should go face him and get it over with, since Nate was still quiet. "I've got to go, Mom. I'll call you later."

"Take care, and give Nate a kiss for me," her mom said.

"I will. Bye." Violet hung up, got out of bed, and wrapped a robe around herself. She took a second to peek at Nate, but he was still sound asleep, so she closed his door and went down the steps.

When she reached the bottom, a heavy hand clamped over her mouth and her back was forced against a large body. She reacted immediately to break his hold. She slammed her head back, hoping to catch him in the nose, but he was so large her head only made contact with his shoulder. Next, she stomped her heel down on his foot, but she was barefoot, and he was wearing boots. With a malicious chuckle, the man lifted her from the floor, proving his strength.

"Stop struggling, or I'll have to hurt you," a voice with a thick Russian accent said in her ear. "And I don't want to do that... yet." He pulled her back against him even more tightly, and she knew no defensive moves or screaming would help her. She could only pray that Nate wouldn't wake up.

It was barely light out when Anderson left the house. He needed to move to process the thoughts in his head. The conversation with Violet the night before had been brutal and raw, and he had no idea how to react other than what he'd said to her. He'd given her and Nate what he could, and he had nothing more in him. He was sure of that.

But, Jesus, she'd shocked him to his core with her declaration of love. He'd been too stunned to move, pinned down with an emotion he couldn't name. All he could think to do was extract himself. And he would do that later today. He'd make sure she and Nate had a clear way back to her house. Hell, he'd buy her a new car himself. He wanted them to be safe. He just couldn't be with them.

As he turned the first corner, he forced himself to focus on his patrol. He'd been careful not to walk the same pattern each morning, but he always accomplished the same goal. He started close to the safe house, checking the streets, and moved outward in a widening circle. He'd been attuned to black SUVs over the past days, but out of habit he looked for anything unusual.

Well… anything unusual for a neighborhood with some definite quirks.

Despite the turbulent night he'd spent, he couldn't forget what Violet had said while they ate dinner. At first, he'd dismissed her concern that the takedown had been too easy, but the more he thought about it, the more he wondered if she was right. She was a hell of an analyst—he knew that from experience. So he'd stay on his guard. Before he sent her and Nate home, he needed to be sure there was no lingering threat against them.

"Good morning, Anderson," Kelly called from across the street. She and Evie were out for their morning powerwalk. He encountered them nearly every day as they made a circuit of the neighborhood. "You had some excitement at your house."

Both women crossed the street to intercept him. He wanted to run for it, but he held his ground. "We did, but it's all fine now." He gave them an easy smile to suggest his words were true.

"We were worried when the police pulled up," Kelly said. "Nothing like that ever happens in this neighborhood."

"I guess the guy had left something hidden in the house when it sat empty, and he came back to retrieve it. We surprised him as much as he surprised us." Anderson had prepared the explanation in advance, just in case.

"What had he left?" Evie asked.

"The police didn't tell us, but I'm guessing it was something illegal." He figured that was a believable comment.

"I'm glad you were there and Violet wasn't home alone," Kelly said with a shiver. "How is she? Better?"

"All recovered," he said, feeling genuine relief. He worried about Violet. A lot.

"That's good. I'm making lasagna tonight. How about if I make an extra for you and Violet?" Evie was smiling at him, expecting him to accept.

"Thanks, but that's not necessary," he said, not even sure they would be in the house by evening.

"Are you sure? Being a new mom can be so tough," Evie said. "My daughter had her first baby last year. Her husband is great and all, but she still struggled."

Was Violet struggling? She'd admitted that she'd had some tough moments with Nate, but what did these women see that he hadn't?

"And being sick on top of that," Kelly added, "makes it so hard."

He blinked at the women, realizing that they genuinely cared. He'd been annoyed at their nosiness, but they seemed to have a real interest in him, Violet, and Nate. He wasn't used to such neighborly behavior, and it still surprised him.

"It's been rough at times," he agreed, "but I guess that's normal, right?" They both smiled at him.

"Maybe you should take her a little treat today," Kelly suggested. "I wish I'd baked some muffins."

"You know, there's that new bakery just up around the corner," Evie said, pointing in the direction that Anderson had been headed. "The bagels are delicious, and the pastries are divine. I'll bet she'd love something from there. Okay, we better keep walking. Oh, and Anderson, pick up some extra bagels and keep them in the freezer.

A frozen bagel is great for a teething baby to chew on. Grandma trick."

"Thanks," he called after them, annoyed with himself for not having noticed what they had. He'd known Nate was cutting teeth, but while he'd been aware of the drooling and crankiness, he hadn't bothered to look for a solution. Why not? That's what he'd have done in any other situation.

And Violet. He started walking. He'd get bagels, make a pot of coffee, and have a conversation with her and say... what would he say? His feet slowed.

He'd say that he appreciated everything she was doing for their son. All right, that was a start, but was that it? Was that all he felt for her? Gratitude?

He imagined going back to his house by himself, and he didn't like how it felt. It seemed lonely, empty. He'd enjoyed living by himself. It proved that he had the means to own a decent home bought through his own hard work. But what if he could have more? What if he could help Violet make a life for their son?

He'd offered her financial support, but that was the easy way out. She needed more from him. She needed emotional support. She needed someone to be there at three in the morning when Nate was fussy. He thought about how he'd stood next to Nate's crib in the night, just watching the baby sleep. It had given him a sense of peace, knowing his son was safe. But he'd also felt a terrible sense of loss, since soon Nate wouldn't be his anymore.

And the temptation to crawl into bed next to Violet had almost overwhelmed him. He'd had to force his feet to pass her door. He'd wanted to make love to her... because he loved her. The force of his feelings made him stop in the middle of the sidewalk. He looked around at the nearby houses with their perfect lawns. It was an odd place to realize he'd fallen in love with Violet, but better there than not at all. And he wasn't going to deny it to himself or to her.

He had to tell her. He had to apologize and hope she loved him enough to take a chance on him. As a partner and father, he wasn't going to be perfect. Far from it, probably. But, dammit, he'd be there for his family.

He hurried on, reaching the bakery just as it opened for the morning.

18

Anderson dug in his pocket when his phone buzzed as he was walking home from the bakery. He checked the screen, a small part of him hoping that Violet had reached out to him. But he saw it was Allen Zimmerman. He answered and kept moving.

"Hey," Allen said. "You home?"

"No, why?" An edge to the other man's voice made Anderson tense.

"Something weird with the security system. We show an exit at 6:10…"

"That was me. I rearmed it when I went out." Anderson had been careful to do that every morning, and he hadn't been about to stop just because they'd captured the assailants yesterday.

"Yeah, we can see that, but the whole thing went offline ten minutes ago. Alarms, cameras, everything. You're not there?" Allen asked again.

"No." Anderson picked up his pace as his instincts started screaming a warning. "I'll be there in two minutes."

"I'll send backup. Be careful," Zimmerman said and disconnected.

Anderson sprinted toward the house but, at the last minute, detoured down an alley. Approaching from the back felt right somehow. He jumped the neighbor's fence and went over a second fence into his yard at a corner of the house where there were no windows. Crouching low, he moved along the side of the building to check the driveway and street, half expecting to see a black SUV. Instead, a blue Dodge Charger he didn't recognize was parked at the curb. It wasn't an unusual vehicle for the neighborhood, but the out-of-state license plates made it stand out.

Could be a coincidence, but Anderson didn't think so.

He worked his way around the house's periphery, looking in windows. The kitchen and dining room were clear, the small foyer and staircase empty. When he reached the living room windows, his heart nearly stopped. Violet sat on the coffee table, her hands tied behind her back with the sash from her robe. A man stood over her. He was in black tactical clothing and had a jagged scar on his cheek.

He was the same man who had come at Anderson when he tried to retrieve the IDs. Anderson took a closer look, and then it clicked. Rafe Solok. Anderson had seen him just once during his time in Moscow. He was one of Volkhov's lieutenants, high up in the Wolf's hierarchy... and a paid assassin.

Solok was talking, but Anderson couldn't hear the words. They weren't important anyway. The important thing was that Violet was still okay... so far. But knowing Solok's reputation, that wouldn't be true for long. And...

Anderson sucked in a breath. Nate. Anderson didn't think for a second that Solok would spare the baby.

No way was he going to lose Violet and his son when he'd just figured out how much he loved them. God, he wished he'd responded differently when she'd poured out her heart the night before. He'd been too stunned, too clueless to realize that being with her was what he wanted. He wasn't having that opportunity ripped away from him.

Anderson needed a plan. Trying to clear his head of emotion, he looked at the situation logically. He had to approach this as if it were a mission. First, he had to get in the house. The French doors that led from the living room to the deck were his best bet. From there, he'd be able to see Violet's face, and Solok's back would be to him.

Keeping his focus on the mission, he noiselessly circled the house until he could see Violet through the doors. Her eyes flicked over him, but she was too smart to give him away. He watched her say something to distract Solok. He almost smiled, so in love with her bravery and her brains.

Violet forced herself not to show her relief when she saw Anderson's face come into view. She didn't waste time wondering how he'd known something was wrong. Since being taken hostage, she'd been paralyzed with fear that he'd come through the front door and never have a chance against Solok.

"Your son is still sleeping? Lucky boy," Solok commented in a casual tone.

Violet swallowed down the bile that rose when he mentioned Nate. It had been unrealistic to hope he was unaware of Nate. "He's with Anderson," she lied. "Far from here." All she could do was pray that Nate didn't wake up and cry.

"Do not try to fool me." Solok waved a gun in her face. "I watched Commander Park leave, and he was alone. When I'm ready, I'll have you fetch the boy. I like families to die together. It makes for such an interesting story in the newspapers."

A chill raced through her, but she had to rely on Anderson to defuse the situation.

"I expect your lover will be home soon," Solok commented.

"We had a fight," she said, telling the truth this time. "He might not come back."

"More lies. I tripped the alarm, so he'll come running back. I'm sure he received an alert on his phone."

She'd forgotten about the security system, but Solok had the details wrong. Rogers's company would get the alarm, which meant they knew of the danger and, presumably, had warned Anderson. If she could just hold out a little longer, Anderson wouldn't have to face Solok alone.

Gingerly, she twisted her wrist, catching the end of the tie that bound it. If she could work her hands free…

Before she could do more, she felt more than saw Anderson's presence in the room. He'd entered through the kitchen and moved without a sound to the living room. His arms were spread wide.

What was he doing? Why hadn't he used the element of surprise to attack?

But she knew why. Even though he didn't love her, he wouldn't put her life in danger.

"Ah, very good. You're back." Solok's smile was predatory. "Why don't you have a seat so we can all… talk."

"I have a better idea," Anderson said, his tone cool. "Why don't you let Violet go and keep me."

"This isn't a negotiation. Sit." The assassin indicated a chair to Violet's left, his gun still trained on her. "Keep your hands on your knees."

Anderson complied and turned to Violet. "Are you all right?"

"For now," she said, her voice steady. As she spoke, she worked the knot behind her back. "You should have stayed away."

"I couldn't," Anderson responded, meeting her eyes.

"How touching," Solok sneered.

"Not at all." Anderson swung his gaze to Solok. "Curiosity brought me inside. I wanted to know why you're pursuing us. I can't quite reason it out."

"Perhaps the analyst can." Solok touched her cheek with one finger.

"I guess I'm not as good as I thought. I have no idea." She kept herself steady despite the vileness of his touch.

"Revenge, of course. The two of you destroyed my life in Moscow, destroyed my family."

"Your family?" Violet prompted, feeling the tie loosen a little more.

"You sent Volkhov to jail. He was… he was like a father to me." He turned away slightly as he spoke, but not enough that she or Anderson could risk a move. "He took me from an orphanage when I was fourteen and turned me into a man."

"I'm sure his prison sentence isn't long." Russian mob bosses never spent more than a few months in jail.

"He's dead." Solok spun back in their direction, his eyes deadly.

"What?" The news shocked her. None of the intelligence she'd reviewed suggested that Volkhov was dead.

"The prison falsified records to hide the truth, but he is dead." Solok looked anguished. "I claimed his body myself."

"That's—" Anderson started.

"We didn't know." She cut him off rather than risk that Anderson's comment would incite Solok. It wasn't time for that yet. She didn't pretend sympathy, but she did want to keep Solok talking as she worked to get her hands free.

"So you see why you have to die," Solok said, his tone sending chills through her.

"A family for a family," Violet spoke quietly as the pieces clicked into place. Her and Anderson's intelligence work had destroyed Volkhov and his syndicate, leaving Solok without a pack, so to speak. His "family" was gone, so he intended to kill hers: the ultimate revenge.

"Da," Solok confirmed with a nod.

"May I ask a question first?" When he didn't object, she went on. "What about the four men who attacked us yesterday? What was the intention with them?"

Solok waved his hand in the air as if dismissing something minor. "Those men were on loan from another syndicate. Disposable."

"So why use them?" she asked, buying time to continue working the knot.

His wolfish smile appeared again. "So that you would think you were free. I like to surprise my prey. I like them to feel that they are safe before I attack."

That explained the ease with which the men had been disarmed. They were sacrificial lambs, perhaps dangerous in their own way—but paid to fail in this case. She'd seen only part of the puzzle the night before. If she hadn't been distracted by the tension between her and Anderson, she might have realized that they'd been lulled into a false sense of security.

She glanced at Anderson. He was coiled like a spring, ready to unwind. At any opportunity, he'd launch himself at Solok—and the assassin wouldn't hesitate to shoot him. She needed another solution. Getting her hands free wasn't enough. She needed a weapon. And then it came to her. Just below where she sat, Anderson had kept a handgun in the coffee table drawer.

She'd objected to it because of Nate, but Anderson had reasoned that the baby wasn't mobile and couldn't get to it. She'd relented... but was it still there? Had Anderson packed up his weapons in anticipation of leaving?

It was a risk she'd have to take. With relief, she undid the last knot holding her hands behind her back. Seeing that her hands were free and seeming to sense she had a plan, Anderson drew Solok's attention to him.

"You'll be captured and tried for murder," Anderson said.

"On the unlikely chance I would be taken into custody," Solok said dismissively, "I would be extradited immediately."

"I wouldn't bet on that," Anderson taunted, leaning forward.

Solok didn't seem unnerved, but he was a tiny bit distracted. She had to seize this opportunity.

Before she could act, Nate cried from his crib. Solok's eyes went to the ceiling, and Anderson leaped forward, driving his head into the Russian's stomach. Solok's gun flew from his hand and spun across the room, out of both men's reach.

Violet opened the drawer and retrieved Anderson's gun, flicking off the safety as she lifted it. The men grappled with each other, making it impossible for her to get a clean shot. She waited, watching for an opportunity. Seconds passed. Solok had height and weight on Anderson, but the SEAL was quicker. When Anderson shoved Solok back, putting some space between them, she took the shot.

The bullet entered Solok's chest high up on the right side. She hadn't shot to kill, but to disable. The Russian staggered and went down. Anderson was immediately on him, flipping him over and yanking his hands behind his back. Solok yelled in pain, but Anderson didn't relent until he had him secured.

Knowing that Anderson had everything under control, she lowered the gun. She was temporarily frozen in place, knowing that she should feel some compunction about shooting a human being. However, she had no regrets and no sympathy for the man who'd threatened Anderson, her, and their son. He would have killed them all. Now that the danger was over, she felt a wave of nerves and nausea roll through her.

Anderson stood and came toward her, but the squeal of tires out front and Nate's repeated cries drove Violet into action. She went to the front door and opened it to signal to Rogers's men that the danger was over. Then, without waiting for them to enter, she took the steps two at a time to reach Nate in his crib.

19

―――――

Violet woke with her head resting on Anderson's chest. His hand was on her waist, and she could hear his slow, steady breathing. It was heavenly to be close to him again, to share a bed with him and know that no one was trying to harm them anymore.

Not long after Rogers's men had arrived the day before, Anderson followed her upstairs, where he gave her a brief, hard hug. He'd taken Nate from her and held him close for a minute before going to deal with the inevitable questions. After that, she'd hardly spoken to Anderson throughout the long day. They passed Nate back and forth as they were interviewed by the local police, state police, and the FBI.

Since Solok was Russian and was wanted for a long list of crimes, the process of questioning was far more complicated than with the four previous goons. She'd spent nearly two hours talking with her supervisor at the agency, conveying every detail of what had happened. She'd gotten only a minor lecture about her break in protocol. Her boss had understood the unusual circumstances. Anderson seemed to have had a similar conversation with his commanding officer, from what she overheard.

By evening they had both been exhausted. After she'd tucked Nate into his crib, she collided with Anderson in the upstairs hall. They hadn't bothered to speak. All that had mattered were their actions. He pulled her into her bedroom, undressed her slowly, and made love to her. It had been both the most real and the most magical experience of her life.

She hated to think what the new day would bring, though. It was so much better to pretend that everything between them was perfect than to face the reality of their lives. Anderson had said nothing to make her believe he'd changed his mind about them and their future. Would Anderson wake up and declare that he wasn't meant for fatherhood after all? Would he see her and Nate home and then leave without a backward glance, as he'd planned before?

She had no way of knowing. For all she knew, spending the night together might have been his way of bidding her goodbye. She sighed, and he stirred at the movement. His hand moved to brush over her hair and resettled around her.

"Good morning," he said, his voice deep and sexy.

"Hi." She turned her face to see his.

"Nate up?" he asked.

"Not yet," she said. They had a few minutes before he would stir. She was looking forward to getting Nate back on a schedule. This whole experience had been hard on him. The question was, would she be parenting alone again?

"We'll have to get moving soon," he said. "It's best if we're out of here before the neighbors start asking too many questions." The gunshot, ambulance, and multitude of law enforcement hadn't gone unnoticed. The neighborhood was abuzz with questions and speculation.

"I know," she agreed, facing the reality that their interlude was over. Anderson was ready to move on, and she had no choice but to do the same. "I have no idea how to explain what happened to the nice people here. They'd be shocked if they knew a Russian assassin visited the street. Maybe I'll send them thank-you notes when I get home."

She waited a heartbeat, then shifted to get up. Despite how much she wanted to stay how they were, it was time she untangled herself from him, physically and emotionally.

"Don't go yet," he said, sitting with his back against the headrest. "We need to talk about what's next."

Here was the moment she'd been dreading, the official parting of the ways. She felt sick just thinking about it, but she forced herself to lay out a logical plan for their separation. "I guess we'll have to travel together until we retrieve your car. Rogers gave me permission to take the one we've been using home until I can make other arrangements."

"We'll need two cars to get home?" he asked, his eyes roaming over her face.

"Well… yeah. I don't live close to you." She realized that he didn't even know what city she lived in. She'd met him at his house when this all began. If traffic was good, it was a two-hour drive from there to her home. "I assume you're going to Hartsville, and I'm…" She trailed off. Was he suggesting they stay together? She touched his chest, her fingers sliding over the hard muscles, before she could stop herself. "Wait, what are you…"

"I want us to live together. I mean, if that's what you want." His expression was serious, maybe even a little worried. "I just don't know which house is best to live at. What do you think? I love Hartsville, and I think it's a safe place to live. On the other hand, my house isn't set up for a baby. You've probably got everything you need at your place, and it's closer to your work, I assume. Maybe you should work up some projections based on the data, so we can make an informed decision."

He kept talking, trying to reason it all out, but she couldn't get past the fact that he wanted to be with her. Did that mean he loved her and Nate? Was he willing to be a family with them?

"We should probably factor crime rates," he continued, "access to medical care, and the quality of school districts into the analysis."

"Anderson, slow down," she managed to say.

"Too soon to worry about schools?"

"Yes, and you've leaped over some data points. Points that I need to make a proper projection."

"Such as?" He grinned at her. Was he teasing her? She couldn't tell.

Nate started babbling in his bed. "Wait here. Don't go anywhere. Please." She touched Anderson's cheek, wanting desperately to kiss him but afraid to trust what he seemed to be saying. "When I come back, we need to backtrack in this conversation, because I'm very interested in gathering the missing data." She got out of bed and yanked on her robe.

In his bedroom, Nate greeted her with a toothy grin. "A tooth," she exclaimed. "Daddy'll be happy to see that finally came through." She quickly changed his diaper and fed him before bringing him back with her to her bedroom. She was a little surprised to find Anderson waiting just as she'd left him. He wasn't the kind to sit around… but she'd given him specific directions and he'd followed them. She smiled.

"Let me." He held out his arms for Nate and settled the baby against his chest. "Now, you." He patted the bed next to him. When she sat, he drew her close to his other side. She felt a soft kiss on her temple and sighed, her body tingling with anticipation. Something very good was about to happen. All the data pointed to it.

"Now, tell me why we're deciding between my house and yours?" she asked.

"Because we have to be together, Violet." Another kiss touched her hair. "I can't live without you."

She tilted her head back to see his face. "That's a big change in your position."

He grimaced. "I was a damn fool. Yesterday morning, I was rushing back here to tell you something important, something I managed to figure out. I hope you'll forgive me for being slow to—" He broke off. "This is all new to me."

"Anderson, I need you to name what *this* is. That's a really valuable piece of information to me."

"I can do that. I love you, Violet." He leaned closer to place one perfect kiss on her lips before continuing. "Like with you, I think it started in Russia, but I shut it down. I've never let myself believe in love or family. Those were things other people had. When you suggested that we could have them, when you wanted them with me, it shook me. I didn't know how to respond." He gave her a sheepish grin. "So I did it badly. I thought you'd be better off if I pushed you and Nate away from me."

"Never," she said, her heart melting at his every word.

"I'm glad you think that, because I can't be without you both," he said. "I'm still not convinced I know how to be a father or that I'll be a decent one, but I'm going to try."

She pointed to where Nate was snuggled against him, thumb in his mouth. "You think that's not proof of your ability to be a dad? Look at him."

"He's beautiful." Anderson's tone was almost reverent. "And so are you. I'm scared that I'm going to screw this up or disappoint you, but I love you too much to do anything but be with you. Can we be together?"

"We can." She put one arm around Anderson and another around their son, feeling that they were truly a family now. "I love you, too, Anderson. You already know that, because I couldn't keep it in even when I should have."

"No, you were right to say it. It was what I needed to hear. You're brave and brilliant and beautiful, and I don't deserve you."

"Stop that kind of talk." She shifted to face him more fully. His expression was so serious that she couldn't resist touching the worry lines across his forehead. "We already know we make a great team. There's no reason to doubt… anything." She smiled at him, enjoying the moment. She kissed him then, letting the kiss communicate her feelings.

The kiss ended when Nate made a gurgling noise and reached out a little fist to grab a lock of her hair.

"I think he's ready for the day," she said, gently untangling herself.

"Then let's take him home."

EPILOGUE

Ten months later

"That's it," Anderson said as he hung the toddler swing from the play structure in his backyard. It was an elaborate fort with a kid-size climbing wall, rope ladder, and slide. Violet had teasingly complained that it was a mini SEAL training ground. Anderson couldn't disagree with her assessment, and he was looking forward to teaching his son some skills.

"Not bad work for a weekend," Patrick commented as he gathered up his tools.

"I appreciate your help." Anderson shook hands with Patrick and Kenton. The three of them had returned from a mission two weeks earlier and were slated to deploy again in a month, so they were all making the most of their time in Hartsville. "One day we'll return the favor, Kenton."

Kenton shook his head. "Not likely, but I'm always happy to help you guys out."

Anderson walked with them to their trucks, thanking them again. After they'd driven away, Anderson went back into the yard by himself. He and Violet had purchased this larger house in Hartsville a few months earlier. After plenty of discussion, they'd chosen Anderson's hometown to raise Nate. Violet had arranged with her agency to work from home, and so far it was pretty damn perfect.

The neighborhood was far nicer than the one Anderson grew up in, and he loved it. Loved the friendly atmosphere, the sense that people looked out for each other. That eased his mind when he was gone on missions and had to leave his family behind.

His family. The expression still surprised him sometimes, but he was ready for the next step, which he planned to take that day. He patted his pocket, assuring himself that the small box was still there. So many times in the past weeks he'd come close to proposing to her, but he'd wanted the timing to be just right.

He eyed his backyard. He'd made sure the setting was perfect for the occasion. Flowers were blooming in riots of white, yellow, and pink. A soft scent perfumed the spring air, which was warmed by mellow late-afternoon sunshine. The only things missing were Violet and Nate.

As if on cue, they appeared on the back deck. Nate had short toddler legs, but that didn't slow him down. When Violet put him down in the grass, the boy ran toward Anderson and his new play structure.

"Do you want to try out the swing?" Anderson asked, scooping his son up and swinging him in a circle. After he'd let himself be a dad, it was like bands had been released from his heart. He didn't always get things right with Nate, but he was trying.

"Yeah," Nate squealed.

"Here you go." Anderson lowered Nate into the bucket-type swing and gave it a push, setting it in motion. Nate's smile was wide, which was more thanks than Anderson needed for the work he'd put into the structure.

"I think he likes it," Violet said, coming to stand next to Anderson. She still took his breath away with her bright, soulful eyes and the way her hair swung loose around her shoulders. "What a treat to have this in his own backyard. He doesn't know to thank you, but I do."

"He's my son. Isn't this what dads do for their kids?" Anderson asked. Nate was a constant source of fascination for him. What always mystified Anderson was how much Nate changed while he was away on missions, even short ones.

"See, I knew you'd figure it out. As a matter of fact, I was so confident that I started making a change to an important document," she said, smiling.

"Oh, what?"

She pulled an envelope from her pocket and handed it to him. "Nate's birth certificate. I want him to legally be Nathan Anderson DiPaula *Park*."

Anderson unfolded the paper and stared at it, speechless. All the details about Nate's birth were there. Date, time, place, mother, and now father.

"It's not a hundred percent official yet," she said. "You have to sign the paperwork, and it has to be returned to the courthouse. But I thought…"

"I'm honored," Anderson managed to get out, so pleased. He knew that Violet trusted him to care for their son, but this felt like a larger declaration of her faith in him as a father.

"I'm glad," she said and gave Nate a push in the swing. "What a perfect day. I love the spring sunshine, and I love having my boys both with me."

Her words jolted him, reminding him that he had a surprise of his own, which he hoped would make the day even more perfect for her.

"I have something for you, too," he said, pulling the box from his pocket and dropping to one knee. She gasped, and when he reached out to her, she willingly put her hands in his. "Violet, you've given me so much. Nate, a life that I never expected, understanding, and so much love. I never want to be without you. So I hope you'll marry me. Will you?"

"Is there really any doubt?" She bent closer, brushing her lips against his. "Of course I'll marry you."

He'd been almost certain of her answer, but he still felt relief flood through him. "Would you like to see the ring?"

She nodded, and he released her hands to open the box. The oval-cut diamond was set in platinum with smaller diamonds encircling it. He'd looked at hundreds of rings before finding this one. Something about it called to him, and he knew it was the one. By the look on her face, he'd been right.

"That's amazing," she whispered. "So gorgeous."

He removed it from the box, and she held out her left hand. When he slipped the ring on her trembling finger, he felt complete in a way he never had before. She turned her hand so the sunlight reflected off the stone, obviously pleased with what she saw.

"Come here," she said in a breathy voice and fisted his shirt front to pull him up.

He put his arms around her, hugging her tight to him. Her hands went to his shoulders, and she tilted her face to his in invitation. He kissed her then, relishing the knowledge that she was his for always.

"When should we get married?" he asked when the kiss ended. He was willing to do the big wedding thing if she wanted it.

"Before you deploy again," she said without hesitation.

"What? In the next month?" He studied her face. He was due on base soon for a mission that was expected to last the summer. That didn't leave much time for planning or a honeymoon.

"Yes. The sooner, the better." She ran her fingers through his hair and tugged him closer for another kiss. "Then, after the wedding, we can get started on a little brother or sister for Nate," she whispered.

"More kids?" The thought should have made him panic. Instead, he welcomed it. And this time he'd be there for Violet every step of the way.

"It's a big house." She tipped her head toward their home. "We should fill it up, and I don't want Nate to be an only child, and—"

"You don't have to convince me," he said. "I'm in."

She smiled at him, love shining in her eyes. He hadn't thought he could be any happier than he was already, but this—their plans for the future—gave him confidence that things were only going to get better from here.

END OF THE SEAL'S SURPRISE BABY

HARTSVILLE'S SEAL HEROES BOOK TWO

PS: Do you love hot blooded SEALS? Turn the page for an exclusive free book offer and exclusive extracts from *The SEAL's Instant Family* and *The SEAL's Surprise Son*.

FREE BOOK OFFER

Read FIVE full-length romances by USA Today best-selling author Leslie North for FREE! Over 600+ pages of best-selling romance with hundreds of FIVE STAR REVIEWS!

Sign-up to her mailing list and get your FREE books

THANK YOU!

Thank you so much for purchasing my book. It's hard for me to put into words how much I appreciate my readers. If you enjoyed this book, please remember to leave a review. Reviews are crucial for an author's success and I would greatly appreciate it if you took the time to review the book. I love hearing from you!

You can connect with me on:

MAKE AN AUTHOR'S DAY

There's nothing better than reading great reviews from readers like yourself, but there's more to it than simply putting a smile on my face. As an independent author, I don't have the financial might of a big NYC publishing house or the clout to get in Oprah's book club. What I do have, as my not-so-secret weapon is you, my awesome readers!

If you enjoyed this book, I'd be incredibly grateful if you could leave a quick review. No matter the length (short is fine!), your review will help this series get the exposure it needs to grow and make it into the hands of other awesome readers. Plus, reading your kind reviews is often the highlight of my day, so please be sure to let me know what you loved most about this book.

ABOUT LESLIE

Leslie North is the USA Today Bestselling pen name for a critically-acclaimed author of women's contemporary romance and fiction. The anonymity gives her the perfect opportunity to paint with her full artistic palette, especially in the romance and erotic fantasy genres.

Find your next Leslie North book visit LeslieNorthBooks.com or choose:

PS: Want sneak peeks, giveaways, ARC offers, fun extras and plenty of pictures of bad boys? Join my Facebook group, Leslie's Lovelies!

BLURB

Navy SEAL Kenton Fitzpatrick has his life planned out. Retire from the military in a few years, find a lovely woman, get married, have kids. But all that gets thrown off when he comes home from a mission ahead of schedule and finds a beautiful woman with toddler twins and a slobbery dog living in his house. Mia Kingston, who gained custody of her nieces when her sister died, lost her apartment in a fire, so Kenton's mom thought it would be fine for her to stay in his house while he was deployed. Though having a family living with him isn't ideal, Kenton agrees to let them stay. With his life plan set in stone, he has no worries that a free spirit like Mia will throw him off track. But when an enemy from Kenton's past surfaces looking for revenge—and puts Mia and the twins in his sights—Kenton may have to accept a change in plans.

Mia always intended to return to her apartment once repairs were completed. And she never intended to fall for a sexy SEAL. Then again, even with the chaos of the twins, the threats on their lives, and Kenton's frustrating need to plan *everything*, Mia's never been happier. Having lost her parents at a young age, it's nice to have a family—even if it's not quite real. While Kenton's focused like a laser on keeping them all safe, Mia's struggling to keep her heart safe from falling too hard, too fast.

Will it take nearly losing Mia for Kenton to realize he can't live without her?

Grab your copy of *The SEAL's Instant Family*
www.LeslieNorthBooks.com

EXCERPT

Chapter One:

Kenton Fitzpatrick closed his laptop and eyed the men who sat across from him. Patrick and Anderson were integral members of the SEAL team he captained—and his two closest friends.

"I'm not satisfied with what happened," he said with a shake of his head. The higher-ups weren't pleased with his team's performance, either, so he'd taken some heat. Not something he was accustomed to. "I want a do-over."

The mission to North Africa to take down a child-trafficking ring had been at best partially successful. Kenton's team had managed to disrupt, but not destroy, the network that brought in children from all over the world and sent them back out to fates he didn't want to contemplate.

"Not likely for us," Patrick said, leaning back in his chair. "But another team will get assigned to finish what we didn't."

"Maybe they'll have better luck," Anderson said.

"Luck has nothing to do with this kind of work," Kenton said flatly. He snatched a pen off the table and clicked it while he thought. It was true that occasionally his SEAL team caught a break, but success came from meticulous planning and flawless execution. He excelled at the former and was well known for it. And he couldn't fault his men's actions. They'd done what he'd planned, but the trafficking ring's leader had slipped through their grasp. Kenton didn't think it would be long before Marcus Ocampa built another network to prey on innocent children. And that pissed him off.

"I'm still trying to sort out exactly where it went wrong," Anderson said. His language skills and analytical brain had been invaluable during the mission, but nothing had been enough to get the team to their end goal.

"Me, too." Kenton needed to think about it more, mull it over. Maybe then it would come to him. He wanted to know what his mistakes had been, so he could avoid them in the future. "I appreciate you guys sticking around to help me finish up." Anderson and Patrick had stayed on base an additional two days, answering questions alongside him and helping him complete the reports when they could have gone home to their families.

"No worries. I can't imagine having one of my kids taken from me and exploited like that," Patrick said with a shudder. He was the father of an eight-year-old girl and a baby boy. "It makes me want to hold my kids close and never let them out of my sight."

Anderson nodded his agreement. He'd married just prior to deploying on this mission, and he and his wife already had a little boy.

"I'll bet your families are anxious to see you. Have you talked to them since we got stateside?" Kenton asked, feeling guilty that they'd lost out on time with their wives and kids.

"Early this morning. They're fine." Patrick grinned. "It'll be complete chaos when I get home."

"You love it," Kenton said.

"I do," Patrick was quick to say. "You'll have to try it sometime."

"I'll get there eventually." Kenton said. He had definite ideas about his future, and kids were part of it, he'd realized in recent months. He already had a house he loved. It was a recent purchase, but he felt sure it was the place where he'd bring his bride. First, he had to meet the right woman, and then, when the time was right, they'd have a couple of kids.

"Eventually is never how it happens," Anderson said with a laugh. "Some woman's going to burst into your plans and change everything."

"You got that right," Patrick agreed. "Just prepare yourself to catch her when she falls into your life, because you won't get any warning."

That seemed to be the way of it with his friends and SEAL teammates. Most had paired off in recent years and were busy raising families. Still, Kenton didn't think a woman was going to land on his doorstep like his buddies seemed to think.

"I've got to be home long enough for that to happen." If he wasn't deployed, Kenton advised other teams about to head out. It was a life that kept him out of the country or on base the majority of the time, which was why he was looking forward to heading home. He had an extended leave coming, and he planned to take it. He wanted to take care of some projects around the house, but his true goal was to lay the foundation for his future. And that meant finding a woman to share it with.

Kenton's phone screen lit up again with another message from his mother. Margaret Fitzpatrick was the most persistent woman he'd ever known. He'd texted her earlier in the day that he'd be headed home soon, and she'd sent him five messages since asking him to call.

"You should call or text your mom back," Anderson said, reading the screen from across the table. "You know how she is."

The three of them shared a grin. Margaret had been a mom to all of them since Patrick's had walked out when he was a kid, and Anderson's was never much interested in parenting. Margaret had been the one who made sure they all had Halloween costumes when they were little and got home from football practices in high school. She was a mother hen who didn't put up with any nonsense.

"Later," Kenton said. "She probably just wants to invite me to dinner. I'm not feeling it."

"You've got to let the mission go," Anderson said, standing up. "We've analyzed it. Viewed it from every angle. What happened wasn't your fault, man."

"I'm not convinced of that yet," Kenton said. The sense of responsibility stayed with him as they drove off base and headed for Hartsville. Kenton dropped off Patrick first, at his house just outside town, and watched as his friend was engulfed in hugs from his wife and kids. Next, he took Anderson to a home in a newer development.

The porch light was on, and Violet immediately stepped outside with their son Nate on her hip and a huge smile on her face.

Kenton beeped his horn as he drove off, happy that his friends had each found a mate who suited them, even if both of them had fallen into relationships in unusual ways. A few minutes later, he turned onto the tree-lined street where he lived. He'd bought the home, sight unseen, eighteen months ago, when he was on the other side of the globe. He'd viewed pictures on the internet and had his family's assurance that he'd love it. And he did. More than he could put into words.

The dark blue Victorian was stately and graceful, the kind of place that exuded comfort and security. It was exactly what he wanted. Patrick and Anderson had teased him about the ornate trim, stained-glass transom window, and rounded turret. He'd taken the ribbing while thinking that his future wife, whoever she was, would appreciate those details.

As he pulled into his driveway, he was just glad to be there and have time and space to himself. He'd call his mom in the morning, but he wanted to sleep in his own bed first. Unpack and unwind before having to socialize. That was always best when he came off a mission. He needed time to adjust to the civilian world.

He grabbed his duffel bag, pausing when he heard a dog bark. He listened more closely. The twilight air was still and quiet, with only the hum of the cicadas and the slight puff of an early autumn breeze in the trees. He waited, and the bark came again. He could have sworn the sound was coming from inside his house, but his ears must be playing tricks on him. He loved dogs, had even gotten interested in training them in the military, but he hadn't owned one since he was a kid.

With a shrug, Kenton let himself into the mudroom and dropped the duffel on the floor. A scrabbling of paws on the tile floor was his only warning before a large dog slammed into him, knocking him off balance and pinning him to the wall. The dog's head was against Kenton's chest. It didn't move to bite him, but Kenton felt the heat of its breath and heard a low growl from its throat.

What the hell! What was a dog doing in his house?

Before Kenton could attempt to shove the dog away, a baseball bat was thrust into his side. Shit. Had he entered the wrong house somehow? His fist clamped around the key he still held. No, he'd let himself in. Before he could say anything, the pressure left his side as his attacker changed strategies and swung at his head. He parried instinctively and caught the bat before it connected, but he couldn't prevent the glancing hit to his shoulder.

He gripped the bat and wrenched it away from his assailant. At the same time, he pushed off the wall, shoving the dog back even as his senses processed who he was up against. He squinted, trying to make out a shape in the shadows. The figure was tall, but curvy. Not what he'd have expected. And he caught the faint whiff of perfume in the air.

A woman? The realization made him hesitate. He'd have had a man on the floor in no time, but…

"What are you doing here?" The voice was feminine but pitched low and threatening. Kenton would be impressed with her bravery if he weren't so damn annoyed to find someone in his house.

"This is my house," he ground out. The dog retreated from him and went to her. "What the hell are *you* doing here?"

No answer came, but a blast of light from overhead illuminated the space. She'd flipped on the old fluorescent bulb that hung above them.

"Holy hell," he said under his breath when he caught sight of her. She was beautiful, beyond beautiful. Her dark blonde hair was streaked with golden highlights, and her eyes were green like summertime leaves. A smattering of freckles covered her nose and cheekbones. And her mouth was lush, deep pink, and made for kissing. He hadn't been wrong about the curves, either. Her breasts were full and round under her tight-fitting shirt, but her waist was narrow and her legs long. And they were fully on display in the yoga pants she wore.

She wasn't eye level with him—few women were—but she was taller than average. The fleeting thought that she'd fit just right against his large frame came and went in his brain in the split second they evaluated each other.

Her chin came up, a look of challenge on her face, and she continued to hold the bat clutched in front of her, long lashes blinking over her eyes. He needed to speak, but he was still taking in the sight of her.

Her lips parted, but before she could speak, the sharp cry of a child came from overhead. A kid? There was an unknown woman, a dog, *and* a kid in his house? What alternate universe had he walked into?

"Oh, damn," she muttered.

Grab your copy of *The SEAL's Instant Family*
www.LeslieNorthBooks.com

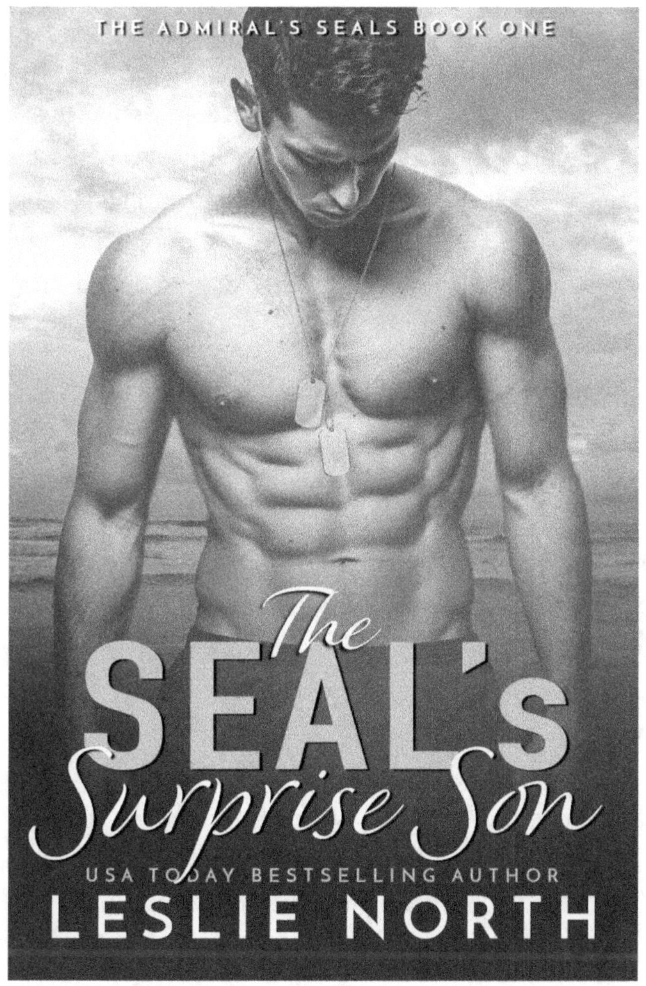

BLURB

Carolyn Evert couldn't take the constant worry and stress that came with having a Navy SEAL fiancé, so she broke it off…then realized she was pregnant. After radio silence greeted her repeated attempts to inform Zach of the pregnancy, Carolyn moved on with her life. Little Austin is happy and healthy, and while she hates the idea of him growing up without a father, she's determined to safeguard the jewelry store her mother founded and make sure Austin never feels unwanted. But everything changes when the store is robbed at gunpoint. Carolyn outwits the robber and defuses the hostage situation—then in strides Zach as part of the security response team. Zach quickly makes it clear he had no idea about the pregnancy, and Carolyn eventually agrees to let him into their son's life…but she's a lot more hesitant about letting Zach back into her own heart.

Zach Vale won't let anything keep him from being the best dad he can be. If Carolyn wants nothing to do with him, he'll live with that. But he can't help but want to protect her and their son. It soon becomes apparent the robbery isn't an isolated incident—and more than Carolyn's business is in danger, especially when she insists on investigating the robbery herself. As she works to solve the mystery of who's behind the vicious attacks, Zach works to make himself part of their lives *and* keep them safe. After all, he's still in love with Carolyn, and maybe if he can be her hero for once, he can convince her to give him another chance.

**Grab your copy of *The SEAL's Surprise Son (The Admiral SEALs Book One)* from
www.LeslieNorthBooks.com**

EXCERPT

Chapter One

"Just sold an engagement ring." Jenna poked her head in the office of All That Sparkles.

"Awesome." Carolyn Evert looked up from the spreadsheet she was studying. "Which one?"

"The one carat heart-shaped diamond set in platinum." From the smile on Jenna's face, she was pleased with herself—and she should be. Both her commission and the store's profit would be very nice.

"I love that one." Carolyn sighed. "It's so romantic."

The ring had only been on display since the store reopened a week ago. Now that the remodel was complete, the neutral cream colors were gone. In their place Carolyn selected soft gray walls, chrome-edged glass display cases, modern recessed lighting, and pops of a vibrant blue for accent. The store did indeed sparkle.

"The couple looked at it yesterday," Jenna said with a knowing grin. "I knew they'd be back."

"You can always peg them. Congratulations."

"Do you want me to start the closing procedure?" Jenna asked.

Carolyn checked her watch. Ten minutes to close. "Sure. That'll be great. I want to get out of here on time tonight."

"Got it." Her most experienced salesperson scooted back out the door.

The thought of how the ring's sale would help the month's bottom line brought a smile to Carolyn's face as she returned to the spreadsheet. Her monthly expenses for All That Sparkles were significantly higher now due to a loan for the remodel and higher security costs.

She'd disagreed with her mother about the expense. And maybe she was taking a chance, but she subscribed to the theory that you have to spend money to make it. The interior of a jewelry store reflected its reputation and merchandise, she felt. Her mother had relented since she'd entrusted the store to Carolyn, who now held the reins.

Carolyn owed her mother so much. Faith had founded the store after Carolyn's father all but abandoned the family. Her hard work had put the business on the map in Sheridan Falls. Carolyn was in awe of someone who could do all that single-handed and raise two daughters, and she felt the pressure of measuring up to her mother's standard as she faced a similar life as a single mom and business owner. Her best efforts might not be enough even with the assistance of dedicated employees—but her self-doubt hadn't prevented her from taking a leap with All That Sparkles.

She heard the click of the alarm. Someone was being let into the office area of the store. A state-of-the-art security system had been an integral part of their refurbishment. It made her insurance company happy and gave her peace of mind, plus, it allowed them to carry top-end merchandise, such as the engagement ring Jenna was celebrating. It was worth it, she thought, even though she grimaced every time she pulled up the expenditures page.

"Mama," her son's voice called, bringing an instant smile to her face. A second later her babysitter entered the office with Austin on her hip, squirming to get down.

"Hi, baby." Carolyn took her fourteen-month-old son, hugging him tight to her and pressing her face into his thick dark hair that was so like his daddy's. With his deep blue eyes, no one could doubt who his father was, not that Zach Vale apparently cared. She suppressed a sigh. Silence had greeted her letters and communications to her ex-fiancé telling him that she was pregnant. After sending one last notification of Austin's healthy entrance into the world, Carolyn had stopped trying to contact Zach, who was off on a mission with his SEAL team. She couldn't change that, so she focused on her son. "Did you have fun today?"

Austin gave her a grin and showed her a toy tractor he had clutched in his hand, zooming it up her arm.

"He's been looking forward to coming all day," Nina said, dropping the bag of baby supplies on a chair. "He loves being here, and he loves his mama."

"Thanks for bringing him to me." Carolyn gave her son a kiss before setting him on the carpet to play. She'd felt guilty about working long hours while the store was being refurbished, because she had promised herself she would never let him feel abandoned by a parent. Nothing she'd ever done to get her father's attention had been enough. She'd tried desperately for years working to be the best student and best athlete, hoping he'd notice. She'd even begged her mother for martial arts classes because her father mentioned that he liked martial arts. She took classes for years, increasing her skill and moving on to grade after grade. Her father never once came to see her demonstrate her skills. Nothing had ever worked to get his attention.

She'd never let her son feel as she had, which might be a struggle down the road. Eventually, she knew Austin would ask about his daddy. All kids did. Whatever she decided to tell him, she'd be careful to never let it seem that he'd been unwanted.

"No problem," Nina said. "I love the new look of the store. The blue sets everything off. On our way here, we took a little stroll past Castle Jewels."

"Oh?" Carolyn's primary competitor had recently updated as well. "Is it nice?"

"Classy looking. Lots of gold accents. But it was kind of stuffy, too. I didn't feel like I could wander in and browse." Nina wrinkled her nose. "I think you made the better choice."

"Hope so." She watched Austin, who played with the tractor, running it over the pattern in the carpet and making goofy faces and sounds. He was so like his father, who despite being a SEAL had loved the silly side of life, too. It had been her choice to end their relationship, but she couldn't help missing Zach. There had been a lot to love about him.

"I've got to get going," Nina said. "My boys have a baseball game tonight."

"I'll let you out through the secure door." Carolyn scooped Austin up and led the way to the showroom.

Just as they reached it, the front door flung open, slamming against the wall, and a man burst through, gun in hand. Carolyn froze in place, hoping this wasn't what it looked like.

"This is a robbery," he yelled, swinging his gun in an arc to encompass the store. "Hands where I can see them."

Carolyn took in a sharp breath, fighting the panic she felt. If the robber had entered five seconds earlier, she could have secured her son and Nina in the office, but they were all too visible. She pressed the tiny button on the key she always carried, triggering a silent alarm that contacted the police and her security firm. It also gave them a live audio and video feed.

"Everybody, down on the floor," the robber commanded. "Except you." He pointed to Jenna, who stood behind a display of their most expensive pieces.

Carolyn gestured for everyone to comply. It seemed safest to obey him while they waited for help to arrive. On her way down, she grabbed a pair of ear protectors left over from the remodel and slipped them on Austin's head. Maybe if her son couldn't hear the drama unfolding in front of them, he wouldn't be frightened. She smiled at him, whispering they were playing a game, hiding the fear that raced through her.

The robber, focused on shouting at Jenna to dump trays of diamonds and sapphires into a bag, didn't notice what Carolyn did or that she and Nina tried to cover Austin with their bodies. If the man walked closer, he'd see the boy, but she'd do whatever was necessary to protect him.

She took a quick look around. Her other salespeople were on the floor, following procedure. They'd gone through training for this scenario, but these situations could go wrong very quickly. *Please let him get what he wants and get out,* she prayed. She winced at the sound of glass shattering as he smashed a display case of emeralds and shouted for Jenna to pick out the precious stones. Jenna worked quickly, filling the bag the robber held.

"Now, you get on the floor, too," he told Jenna, "and the rest of you stay down." He moved toward the door. It was going to be over more quickly than she'd expected. A few more seconds and he'd be out.

Carolyn tensed as the robber swung the heavy glass door open, revealing a swath of the street from where she lay. Police cars blocked the street. They'd arrived silently, which was protocol, but she could see the man panic at the sight. His means of escape was cut off.

He pivoted his head like an animal who had unexpectedly become prey to a larger beast before stepping back, slamming the door, and throwing the dead bolt. They were trapped in the store with an armed robber. The gun he carried swept across all of them, shooting fear through her heart.

Zach Vale attached the scope to his sniper rifle after taking up position on the second floor of a building directly across the street from All That Sparkles. The situation was going to challenge the calm persona he'd mastered as a sharpshooter on his SEAL team. He reminded himself that it was a job like any other. He didn't want to screw it up, and he sure as hell didn't want to tell his new boss the store he was watching through his scope belonged to his former fiancée. He'd get replaced by another sharpshooter ASAP—and no way was he letting someone else take his spot on this mission. Carolyn might have tossed him out of her life, but he'd do whatever he could to protect hers.

He evaluated his line of sight into the store. If the target showed himself in the front window, he'd be easy pickings. Zach used the scope, hoping to catch sight of the man. Nothing.

He didn't know if Carolyn was in there. It was likely, all his experience with her told him that. She prided herself on working hard. That was unlikely to have changed in the nearly two years since she'd ended their engagement.

He could barely think about that night. He'd had no warning. She'd simply told him it was over because she could no longer take it that he chose his work as a SEAL over her. Never much of a talker, he'd been knocked speechless by her declaration. He'd thought what they had was special, the kind of love that could weather any storm. How wrong he'd been still stunned him. He should have known that type of love didn't truly exist.

To have Carolyn disrespect his job in the Navy—when he was convinced it had saved him from a life of crime—had sliced through him, and he'd been powerless to argue with her rejection. He'd thought she knew him well enough to understand his position as a sharpshooter was like breathing to him. How could she not have seen that giving him an ultimatum about his job was like asking him for his lungs?

"Vale, do you have a good position?" The sharp voice of his commanding officer came through his earpiece.

"Roger that. Front window is in range. I can take him if he shows."

"Stand by. Let the negotiator do his job, but don't let your guard down."

As if Zach would in any situation, let alone when the woman he'd once loved was likely feet from an armed robber. He pushed away the memory of Carolyn and their broken engagement. He had a job to do. He refocused, digging deep for the calm that was necessary to pull the trigger. Chatter on the radio told him negotiations weren't going well. The robber wouldn't speak to the police negotiator on the phone, the standard way of communicating in these situations.

Zach didn't want to think about how desperate a man had to be to refuse a simple conversation, even if it was to tell the negotiator to go to hell. He wished he had the visual and auditory feed his commander did. Then he could be sure where Carolyn was. But all he had were his own eyes trained on a shiny glass window. He'd chosen his position because the glare was minimal, but it would still be a factor if it came to eliminating the target.

"In the window," Zach heard on the radio, but he'd already made visual contact through his scope. The robber's shoulder came into view: gray T-shirt, nothing remarkable, but he seemed to be dragging something. Zach increased the pressure on the trigger, waiting for more of the target to show. He almost had a clean shot when a blond woman appeared in front of the man. His hands gripped her arms, pressing into her flesh and holding her in place in front of him.

She clutched a kid to her chest, her hand wrapped around his head. The boy was young, barely more than a baby, and wore red ear protection. Zach mentally cursed the robber for hiding behind a woman and child.

Although he already knew what he would see, Zach focused the scope on the woman's face to confirm her identity. Carolyn. Her brown eyes were wide in fear, and there was no sign of the dimples he'd always loved so much. He released his trigger finger as his breath caught in his chest. He'd never attempt the shot.

"Human shield," he said into his mic. "No clear target."

Grab your copy of *The SEAL's Surprise Son (The Admiral SEALs Book One)* from
www.LeslieNorthBooks.com